Those of the Realms

HELL

JOEY ZIGAN

ISBN 979-8-88540-968-1 (paperback)
ISBN 979-8-88540-969-8 (digital)

Christian Faith Publishing
832 Park Avenue
Meadville, PA 16335
www.christianfaithpublishing.com

Printed in the United States of America

PROLOGUE

A golden, blinding light shone all about them. Tendrils of a shimmering bronze glow enveloped everything in sight. To those unaccustomed, it would mean instant death. But to these, it was everything—the very air they breathed. A truer, more satisfying air than anything they had experienced before. The group sat around a table to rest. There was no need for food or drink; they were sustained by something that had no end. All the same, though, they were enjoying a meal together as they reminisced. The group had heard a tale from a man they met during their travels. He told them of surreal landscapes and shapes they had never imagined. Where he was from, the concepts of physical and spiritual were one and the same. The group struggled to understand his tale as best they could, drawing what parallels they could to their own lives. The man also told them of a colossal horror that stalked his land, seeking unwitting prey to devour. To the group, such a threat seemed an easy danger to avoid, at first. As the discussion went on, however, they began to realize they had experienced the same threat in their own lives. Sometimes they had escaped its clutches, but far more often, they had fallen prey themselves.

One of the men in the group, one with bright hair, was especially taken aback by this realization, "How could I be so blind for so long? Even with the clarity we have now, I continue to make new discoveries every day here."

A young woman addressed his concern, "It's not just you. I think we can all say that every day here brings more and more truths to light that, in hindsight, seem so obvious."

The man continued, "Oh, of course. I completely agree. It's just"—he paused for a moment, trying to formulate the right words—"I guess in my situation, I was so close to that evil for so long it's particularly jarring to only now realize it."

The woman nodded her head, knowing full well what he meant. A youthful, dark-haired man beside her spoke up, "I get it. I think we all can understand that in a way. Maybe some more than others, but I think all of us spent far more time with the beast that we'd like to admit."

The bright-haired man agreed as the youngest boy of the group thought aloud, "It's interesting to me that no matter how he appeared to each of us in our lives, there's a consistent theme as to how he went about his business. Even in a towering, monstrous form, his first priority is always to lead us astray through deception and trickery rather than by intimidation or force."

There was a pause as the group considered this point. A man at the head of the table began to speak at the same time as the man beside him. One of them deferred, and the man at the head spoke, "That's a very good insight, Aadi. You continue to impress me with your quiet wisdom."

The boy shrank a bit in embarrassment even as he thanked him.

The man continued, "It makes me think that his priority wasn't even to ensnare us, not really. That is to say, his ultimate goal is to attack and hurt our Father. And since we are His children, convincing us to commit sins of our own volition makes the acts that much more blasphemous."

The young woman added, "That would help to explain why our instincts were to pass blame whenever we felt shame. Even if it was only partially true, in our fallen minds, the origin of the sin was from Satan and not ourselves. Maybe, on some innate level, we tried to lessen the offense to our Father by making the offense less personal."

The dark-haired man beside her answered, "That would make sense. Though, we know now all too well that sin in all its forms is intensely personal to our Father, I can at least imagine how we might've believed that was possible before."

"Or let ourselves believe it," the bright-haired man added, his head resting in his hand.

The group gave a sympathetic look to the bright-haired man.

Another dark-skinned man who hadn't spoken yet interjected, "Don't think for a second you held a monopoly in that department. We both acted the villain for a time until we were shown the light. And when we were faced with that choice, we chose submission and salvation."

The bright-haired man shot him a smile.

The dark-skinned man continued, "What strikes me the most is the idea that somehow, more than being shown the light, he lived here for longer than we have now and still chose to rebel. I try to understand that even after basking in His presence for millennia, he could still truly believe in his superiority. The depths of his pride seem unfathomable."

After a moment, the man at the head of the table answered, "A part of me pretends to comprehend it. I try to imagine what seething jealousy must boil in his heart at every moment. It has to be a deeply personal and intimate thing in his mind for it to fuel his rage for so long and in spite of everything he's witnessed. To him, it must have been a status he believed he deserved so much that without it, he was willing to throw away everything else he had."

"And continues to believe," The young woman added. "As much as we all love and adore every instant we've been given here, at times, I forget there are still so many more living their lives apart from grace and love. And that threat continues to stalk for a moment of weakness. There are so many more out there being led toward their own demise without even realizing it." Her voice filled with emotion.

The dark-haired man beside her put an arm around her. It was a reality they had all endured and been released from. Until the time had come, though, it would continue unnoticed by far too many. The group's meal continued, still discussing the bittersweet subject. They had finished their own struggles but knew that far too many would be unwittingly led astray and never find the same peace their group had.

ONE

Josep was asleep. As his senses slowly returned to him, he began to stir. He didn't hear the familiar sound of his alarm beeping, but he hadn't for some time. It was a habit for him to set it before bed even though he woke up five minutes prior all on his own. Before he rolled over to grab his watch off the nightstand, he opened his eyes. He could feel her hand holding his. Her warmth was comforting and full of love. She had been the first thing he laid eyes on every morning for so many years now. It was a routine he was overwhelmingly grateful for. For a moment after he'd opened his eyes, he saw her in her youth, but it was just his imagination. In reality, she was a fragile, snow-white woman whose prime had passed long ago. To Josep, though, she seemed all the more radiant than the day he had first laid eyes on her. He laid there longer than he meant to, just staring at her as she slept. The beeping pulled him back to reality, and he moved to turn it off. It took some effort, more than he expected at first. There was nothing strange about the day prior; they had gone to sleep at the usual time after a relaxing day with their family. Today, he was particularly slow, though. He finally managed to get his hands on the device and silence the alarm, but by then his wife was awake. Ashley was not a morning person and never had been. Josep watched with a smile as she stretched, shuffled, and fought back against the day. Slowly but surely, she finally came to and her eyes opened. When she had left her dream world and saw him, the two exchanged a very sleepy "good morning."

Church wouldn't start for a fair number of hours, but it would take them that long to get properly ready. To Josep, the mornings were nothing to shy away from. As he'd grown older, he'd also grown a deeper appreciation for the quiet hours before the world resumed its business. There was a peace in the mornings that he was quite fond of. Despite her apparent resistance, though, he knew Ashley, and somehow, she always managed to get herself ready and at the door in time to leave. Josep sat up at the edge of the bed, taking his time as he went. The aches and pains that were, at this point, like old friends, slowly settled into their proper places. He yawned long and deep. Before standing up, he instinctively reached behind him and patted the pile of sheets a few times. Without looking, he knew that Ashley had resettled herself and was giving in to the pull of sleep again. Sure enough, his makeshift alarm woke her again, and she started the lengthy process of getting up in full.

Josep grabbed his cane that rested against his nightstand and braced himself before rising to his feet. Both he and Ashley had been blessed to be able to take care of themselves even in their old age, without constant care from others. That freedom had given them plenty of time to enjoy the last few years in a similar, albeit slower, way to their first few years together. Now, this morning as every other, Josep scooted himself into the bathroom and began the process of getting ready for the day, with Ashley close behind.

The sun was now shining bright in the sky. It was warm but not quite warm enough to be unpleasant. Their oldest son, Eric, was visiting with his family, so the house was buzzing with activity all morning. The group did eventually make their way to church though they were nearly half an hour late. The congregation was finishing a hymn Josep didn't immediately recognize as he and his family walked in. They made their way to their usual seats as the pastor stood up to begin his message. Josep didn't particularly mind missing the music, but it was peculiar.

Even with company, he and Ashley hadn't been late to church in a very long time. He thought it must be his grandkids taking more energy out of him than he was used to. Fortunately, the youngest of the group was now sixteen. Even so, it was getting to be more than Josep could handle without wearing out. The march of time had taken its toll on both him and Ashley. It wasn't something either of them lamented, simply a reality they were still learning to contend with. They had lived long and full lives. Ever since the day they met, it was like a fairy tale.

When Josep met Ashley, she was a beautiful, young princess. Everyone who met her fell in love with her. She was charming, vibrant, and interesting. She had a certain air about her; people just liked to be around her. Her joy was a constant, nearly tangible thing. To this day, that presence had never left her. If anything, it had only grown more intoxicating. There was just something about her. That joy was something she had shared with her children and grandchildren. To Josep, it truly was idyllic; he had never dreamed of having so much happiness in his life. He had countless things to be thankful for, but above them all was Ashley herself. Never had he dared to even hope for someone as wonderful as she was. A light seemed to glow about her all the time.

They met by complete chance when they were in college, and it was love at first sight. Within a few months of meeting, they were married, and they rode off into the sunset. Now, all these years later, here they sat. Ashley was enraptured in the sermon as she always was. But Josep found himself distracted today. He was particularly pensive, lost in thought, remembering all the times they'd shared together. There was a strange sense of nostalgia and gratitude swirling within him today. Time seemed to whiz by at this point in his life. It seemed he had only been staring at his bride for a few minutes, and the service was over and done.

The church rose to its feet and finished by singing "Amazing Grace" as they always did. However, Josep and Ashley could only stand for a few minutes at a time without moving, or their strength would give out. Josep sat and watched Ashley pack up her sermon notes in between the pages of her Bible. One by one, he looked down the aisle to see his son, his wife, and their children singing. A sense of pride and love filled his spirit. He was truly grateful for what he'd been given. It seemed as if his efforts over the years had paid off, far better than he ever would've imagined as a young man looking to the future. He was now even more excited to spend the day with his family—a quiet gathering together. Fortunately, he and Ashley got to see their kids more often than some other families did. Both of their sons and their daughter lived only a few hours away, at most, and visited fairly regularly. Their visits were something Josep and Ashley cherished more and more the older they got.

All too soon, the song was over, and the pastor gave his closing comments. The group rose to their feet and picked up their belongings. The younger ones were up and gone in a flash, rushing as if to be the first out of the room. Eric and his wife followed after checking to see Josep and Ashley had made it to their feet. Slowly but surely, Josep stumbled down the aisle following his wife. They made their way to the end and were just beginning to join the flow of traffic.

"Ashley! Oh, Ashley!"

Josep recognized the voice of Emma, one of Ashley's more talkative friends. She appeared from somewhere in the bustling crowd. Ashley greeted her as the two exchanged a warm hug.

"Oh, dear, how are you?"

She was a sweet woman but far more chatty than Josep would've preferred. She responded with a bright, chipper voice, "Blessed and happy, sweetheart. I wanted to introduce you to the sweetest young couple that's visiting today." Emma turned back and motioned to a pair that Josep hadn't taken notice of, standing just by the slow river of people that were streaming out of the building. A strapping, young man stood a foot taller than the petite woman that stood at his side. Emma introduced the two, "This is Robert and Cynthia… Stone, right, dear?"

Cynthia responded, "Yes, ma'am. We're new to the area and heard great things."

Ashley chimed in with her usual beaming smile, "Oh, that's wonderful! We're so glad to have you. Do you two know anyone else here?"

"No, ma'am. Total strangers!" Cynthia chuckled to herself, and the old women chuckled back.

Josep caught their names and immediately began to check out of the conversation. He was never particularly social to begin with, and as he had grown older, he had less and less interest in meeting new people. However, he knew Ashley. She had always been a social butterfly and never met anyone she wasn't fast friends with. Josep stood quietly behind Ashley as the group exchanged pleasantries while he half-listened. The couple had moved to the area after Robert got a promotion at his office. Ashley and Emma congratulated him before immediately moving into how long they'd been married and if they had any children. Apparently, the couple was essentially newlyweds; they had been married just under a year at this point. Again, they received a round of congratulations.

"That is all so wonderful to hear!" Emma repeated her enthusiasm, "Well, we are so happy you chose this as the church to try out."

Cynthia answered with a somewhat shy tone, "Well, to be honest, this is the first time we've ever visited any church." She glanced at her husband with a somewhat embarrassed look, like she'd been swept up in the conversation and forgotten herself.

This, however, only redoubled Ashley and Emma's enthusiasm. Ashley spoke up first this time, "Oh, well we are honored! What made you two want to visit?"

Robert answered, "Well, we're both spiritual people, but we've never really been religious before. But as we've been talking about making a family together, we started wondering what options were out there, ya know? And like she said, we heard good things about this place, so we wanted to give it a shot."

"That is just fantastic! Well, if you have any questions or anything, feel free to ask anytime. We are more than happy to have new people."

For a moment, it seemed the conversation would end there as the young couple thanked Ashley and nearly began to take a step back. Josep knew better, though, and his plans of having a quiet family day were all but gone. Ashley continued, "You know, our son and his family are visiting, but if you two don't have any plans, we'd be more than happy to have you join us for lunch! I don't know if you've heard of it, but there's this wonderful little restaurant that we just love. We can get to know you two better and get you more acquainted with the church."

She was just too friendly. It was something Josep had grown accustomed to after so many years. He loved it about her. If anything, he just wished she was this friendly slightly less often. The family's comment about being new to religion was the lynchpin, though. Josep knew Ashley would never waste an opportunity to talk more about how Christ had changed her life. Josep smiled a genuinely friendly but tired smile as the couple agreed to Ashley's proposal; her magnetic personality always won out.

After a few more moments of pleasantries, Ashley said goodbye to Emma, and they went their separate ways. Josep and Ashley made their way out the front door of the sanctuary with their new friends in tow. Eric and his family were piling into the car when they saw the strangers following Josep and Ashley. They introduced the couple and explained the plan to Eric and his wife, and the rest of the day began.

Over the next several hours, the group enjoyed a pleasant meal together, and, as Josep was used to at this point, they all became good friends. Eric and his family had all inherited Ashley's glowing personality, and together, they overwhelmed the young Mr. and Mrs. Stone with a flood of welcoming love. It wasn't something the newlywed couple was used to, but it didn't take long for them to grow attached to it. This was something Josep had seen time and time again. He was proud to see his son and his family continue the legacy of friendly, good spirits to everyone they met. All the while, Ashley shared as much about Jesus as she could. If they weren't enjoying themselves so much, Josep knew it would've been absolutely smothering. Ashley was too passionate, though, and the young couple was entranced. By the end of their time together, there were plans for the Stones to visit their Thursday night Bible Study and the church picnic the following month.

It was late in the afternoon by the time Josep and his family returned home, and before he knew it, the sun had set; and it was nearing the end of the day. Time truly was moving faster and faster it seemed. In the blink of an eye, the night was coming to an end, and Josep was back in his bedroom. Ashley was washing up while Josep reset the alarm on his watch.

"That was so fun with the Stones today, wasn't it?" Ashley spoke from the bathroom.

"Mm-hmm," Josep answered without really thinking.

"Weren't they just adorable? Robert and Eric seemed to get along really well too."

"They sure did." Josep finished and set the watch on his night-stand. He felt an ache in his chest and began to massage it before he noticed Ashley looking at him from the doorway.

"What's the matter?" she asked.

He waved her off, "Nothing, nothing. I'm just tired."

"You sure? You seemed kind of off all day," she said as she finished whatever it was she was fiddling with.

He forced more energy into his answer, "Yes. I promise, dear. I've been tired all day."

"I feel like we've both been tired for a long time now." Ashley chuckled in response.

It was true; more and more every day, it seemed. He continued to idly rub at his chest.

Ashley walked in and began to slowly make her way around the bed. "Did you really like them?"

"Hmm?" Josep refocused his attention.

"I said, did you like them? You didn't really talk to them that much during lunch."

"Yes, yes. They're a very nice young couple." He paused for a moment before continuing, "Honestly, they remind me of us in a way. They seem to really love each other."

She shot a tender smile at her husband. "They really do, don't they? I told them it just keeps getting better and better." She sat down with a thump on the bed.

"It does when you're with the right person." Josep stretched one last time before hitting the light switch above the nightstand.

Ashley reached over and put a hand on his. "And when you focus on what's truly important."

Her hand felt cool on his skin but filled him with familiar warmth. He answered back to the darkness, "That's true too."

Josep settled into his cozy spot on the mattress. Immediately his eyes began to droop. He was particularly tired tonight. He mused into the void, "I guess if you have that you can handle anything." He followed up his idle thought with a big yawn. Ashley answered in kind.

"You tired, sweetheart?" he asked.

Ashley answered with an exaggerated mumble, "Hmm? Mm-hmm."

Josep chuckled back. "Yeah, me too." He stretched his hand out into the sheets searching. It only took a moment for his hand to find hers searching as well. He always slept on his side and she on the other. He gave her a gentle squeeze. "Sweet dreams, Ashley."

She answered in a tender voice, "You too, baby."

A whisper now, as the sleep quickly enveloped him, "I love you."

Her answer drifted into his ear, "I love you too."

Within moments, darkness overtook their minds. They drifted off into a deep sleep. They laid down that night, holding each other's hand as they did every night. Then, smiling as they slept, they breathed their last.

THREE

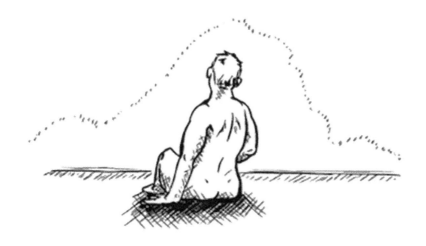

Josep was asleep. As his senses returned to him, he began to notice the blinding light around him. The air was cool and still. He was laying down but not in his bed. The surface he lay on was hard. He could hear the faint sound of wind chimes in the distance. He began to open his eyes. He could only manage it slowly though. It was so bright. When he did finally squint his eyes open enough to see anything, he found himself in a vast white expanse. The stark white floor stretched into the distance as far as the eye could see. The sky was empty. There was nothing anywhere in sight. He snapped awake. His mind began to buzz with unspoken questions, *Where am I? How did I get here?* Then, as he began to look around, a much more urgent question: "Where's Ashley?"

Before her name could leave his mouth, a voice came from behind, "She's not here." He turned around quickly, still sitting on the floor. There was no one there. The expanse continued in all directions. He paused a moment, looking all around.

"Hello? Who's there?"

The voice spoke again as if someone was standing directly behind Josep. The voice was deep and strong, but smooth. "You know, Josep." A thought began to dawn in his mind. He hadn't even considered it, but what else could it be?

He muttered, "Am I—"

"Dead," the voice finished.

Josep's eyes widened slowly as reality washed over him. He was dead, which meant he knew where he was. It had to be; and if it was, then he was all right. Everything was all right. He felt like he was home in a way. It was almost as if he had been there before. It felt somehow familiar. But it didn't last long. There were too many questions. First and foremost, though, "Is Ashley all right? Is she here?"

"No, Josep. She is not here."

"Then, she's still alive?" There was a pause. "Could you somehow comfort her? I don't want her to be sad or to worry about me. She nee—"

The voice interrupted, "She has passed as well, Josep. You both left together."

"But then—" Josep struggled to understand or simply refused to. The thought was born somewhere in the back of his mind. "When can I see her?"

Another pause. "You can't."

The thought began to grow, and that sense of familiarity began to give way to dread. "Why not?"

Another pause. A pause that lasted a lifetime. "She's not here."

That question came to his mind again, and the panic began to take control as Josep found his hands trembling. "Where is she?"

"She's not here, Josep," the voice said, always from behind as if someone was whispering in his ear.

Josep was confused. He couldn't trust what he was hearing. It had to be that the voice didn't understand. "What do you mean? Why not?"

The voice was too calm and collected. So matter-of-factly, "She isn't here, Josep. She has been judged."

Josep struggled for words, "No, i-it can't—she can't be."

The voice was silent as Josep stammered. "You don't understand! She was...she was perfect! She never did anything wrong. She spent her whole life doing what was right. She never hurt anyone. She has to be here! Where else could she be?"

"She's not here, Josep. She never will be," the voice spoke calmly, too calmly.

Josep was spinning around, trying to see something to attach to the voice he was hearing, to the voice that was ending his world. His head was spinning. In his heart, he knew all along. He must have. He never wanted to admit it to himself. He had always convinced himself that there would be more time. There always had been. He had tried to explain to her how she was wrong; how she was close but not quite there. She was just too committed to these little details that didn't matter. Josep knew that was holding her back, but that wasn't enough to condemn her soul. It couldn't be. Josep would have known if it was. He would've done something about it! He would've made sure she knew. There had to be some mistake. For years, she had been the person everyone looked up to. He had always strived to be as good as she was. How could someone like her be...

"This isn't right. This can't be right," Josep was speaking aloud, but it sounded more like he was trying to convince himself. After all, he knew who he was talking to. It couldn't be a mistake...but it had to...it just had to.

Josep was shouting now, a wild rage and sorrow swirling in his chest. "Why! What did she do that was so wrong?"

The voice answered, still calm and collected, "The wages of sin is death, Josep. The consequences of her actions have determined her fate."

Josep was still screaming, emotion flooding every word, "What was so bad that she deserved this, though? She served you for decades! She dedicated her life to doing what was right. She was so good! Isn't that enough?"

The voice was silent. Josep was spiraling with no end in sight. A flurry of sadness turned quickly into anger. He screamed at the sky, louder than before, "She never did anything wrong! How could you—!"

"How could YOU?" The voice cut him off, booming louder than anything Josep had ever heard. The world around him shuddered at the explosive force, and he lost his footing. Josep fell to the floor, tear-filled eyes wide in terror. After a few moments, the echoing subsided, and the voice continued, "You knew. How many moments did you let pass when you could have said something? How many opportunities did you squander? You had her life in your hands, and what did *you* do, Josep?"

Josep was frozen by the voice's words. His lips quivered as the adrenaline coursed through his veins, and his mind raced. A lifetime of memories filled his mind's eye. Moments. So many perfect moments that went by without a word. What was he thinking? He screamed in his mind at the shadows. If only he'd known. Only…he did know. He had always known. He had no defense. He had every opportunity. He had for almost a hundred years. He had thought about it so many times, but he never said anything. Instead, he avoided it his entire life. She brought it up far more than he ever did. Even then, he never took the chance. It was uncomfortable; it always led to an argument. If he'd known it was that important, he would've pushed through for her, though. If he had another chance, he would do it right.

Josep scrambled to his knees and put his head to the floor. "Give…g-give me another chance." Josep stuttered, "I'll tell her. I'll make sure she knows—"

"It's too late, Josep."

Josep was still fighting with everything he had in him, but the despair was growing as quickly as his realization was. He muttered to himself over and over again as he stared at the sterile ground, "She can't be…she can't be…she's not—"

"She is. You must accept it," the voice spoke flatly.

What else was there to say? But Josep wouldn't—he couldn't believe it. There *was* a mistake. There *had* to be. Once more a panic swelled up in him. He couldn't give up. Not now that he knew the truth. He raised his head with tears streaming down his face. "Where is she?" He said the words more than he asked them.

"She's gone, Josep."

His throat began to close up as the tears streamed down his cheeks. His mouth twitched, and his hands were shaking as he tried to fight back the truth. His face was contorting back and forth between panic, rage and sorrow. "Where is she?!"

"Josep…" One word filled with a thousand lifetimes of grief.

He couldn't hold back anymore. He rose spinning, trying to find something, anything to attach the voice to. He wept and screamed and spun around madly, barely able to see anything through all his sorrow and grief. His gasping and weeping choked any words he tried to make into incoherent babble. His mind was so full it was blank. It wouldn't end like this. He wouldn't give up. But his body gave out. No pain he had ever experienced could compare. How could anyone endure such suffering? Despite his best efforts, his legs buckled, and he collapsed to his knees. With every ounce of strength he could muster, he screamed one last roar into the void before all went dark, "WHERE IS SHE?!"

FOUR

S uddenly Josep was in a void of darkness. Shadows swirled around him. He felt as if he was floating. He was in his body but couldn't move the way he wanted. As if in a dream, he was there but not entirely. He could see the floor a few feet below where he was hovering. The ground was rocky and uneven, like a cave. It was far too dark to see anything else, though. A spot in front of him began to twist more intensely. The dark ground sunk into an even darker hole, then from the hole, a silhouette arose. Someone was laying on the ground, seemingly asleep. Josep tried to speak, but his voice eluded him.

Hello? Is someone there?

His words echoed in his mind but couldn't escape his mouth. He felt like a spirit, separated from his body. The figure on the ground began to awaken. They sat up and peered into the inky blackness that surrounded them. Josep couldn't quite make out who or what this figure was until they built up enough courage to whisper into the darkness. A woman's voice, soft and reserved, "Hello?" Josep's heart leaped into action. He knew this voice; it was Ashley. Again, stronger than before, he tried with all his might to cry out to her.

Ashley! I'm here! I'm right here!

But it was in vain. He had no strength to do anything. He could only watch and wish that she could hear him. She had barely made a sound, but in this quiet, it sounded much louder than it was. There was no response for some time. The void was thick with silence until it was interrupted by a loud click and a sudden shower of light from behind. Josep could see Ashley's silhouette turn quickly toward the light. Her back was toward him, and she was facing away toward what they could now see was a doorway. A single dangling light bulb hung inside what looked like a long, dark hallway. She hesitated, but soon Ashley rose to her feet and began to step toward the light. As she made it to the doorframe, she stopped. Josep seemed to move on his own. Or rather, the world seemed to move around him. He had no control at all. He could only watch in silence. Ashley began to step into the hall past the dangling light, but after only a step or two, something unsettling caught her eye. A few more steps down the hall, in one of the corners were scratches in the stone. It looked like something was clawing at the floor, being dragged further in. Immediately, she began to reel backward. In the blink of an eye, there was suddenly someone behind her. If Josep had a heart, it would've burst by now. He was panicked and screaming in his mind to warn her.

Ashley! Look out! No!

She continued to back up until she ran into the looming figure. She froze in terror. The shadowy figure spoke in a deep, smooth voice, "What's the matter, dear? Are you lost?"

She turned around in a panic. Josep was desperate to see her face and for her to see his. But his vision was blurred. The world swirled around him until he was behind her yet again, looking up at the man that was now in front of her. As soon as her eyes met his, his hand was on her throat. She tried to pry his grip loose, but it was like a vice; there was no fighting. He lifted her a few inches off the ground and slowly took a step forward into the light. He stood head and shoulder above her, imposing and muscular, but smooth and beautiful. Silky blond locks reached down to his shoulders.

Even as she pried at his hands, her eyes couldn't leave his. They were dark and deep. His gaze was unyielding. Everything about him was stoic and deliberate—almost regal—but there was something else, something that brought more terror to Josep's soul than anything he had ever experienced. He held her aloft for a few moments before the man spoke, calmly but intensely, "What's with that look? It's almost like you don't recognize me." His other hand came up, and he caressed her cheek with his finger.

Josep swelled with rage and screamed in his mind to no avail.

The man continued, "Oh, sweet thing, I'm hurt. So many years together, and you give me such a cold greeting. After I did all this work preparing you a room, as well. Tsk! Tsk! Tsk!"

Josep could hear Ashley gasping for air. Her movements began to slow as she began to pass out.

"Oh, worry not, princess. You'll be well taken care of." Holding her aloft, the man slowly stepped down the hallway. He seemed to walk right through Josep, and the world swirled again. Josep was at the man's back now, watching as he disappeared into the void, another loud click sounded, and the world returned to blackness.

There were flashes of images in Josep's mind. He saw the man leaving the dark cave. He saw a city of ruined buildings and dark storm clouds. He saw the man walking the halls of a dark and foreboding prison. Then finally, the world swirled again. Now Josep was hovering above a narrow, stone bridge. Dark, evil clouds swirled above and below. Red arcs of lightning streaked this way and that. He saw the man walking across the bridge, a fair distance away. Ashley was dangling limply in his hand. Josep's soul was overcome with an impotent terror and sorrow. The clouds ahead moved aside, and Josep could see at the end of the bridge the silhouette of a building. It looked like a house, but it was too dark to see. He had to save her. She was in danger. He fought with everything he had in him, but it changed nothing. Like a phantom, he simply watched as the world slowly pulled away. Like a dream coming to a close, it all began to blur. A dark fog filled his consciousness, and he returned to an empty sleep.

Josep's eyes snapped open. His heart was still racing. "Ashley!" Silence answered him, and he remembered where he was. He took a minute to try and calm his rapid breathing. As he did, his mind was filled with images of a dark place, of a terrifying man, and of Ashley. After a moment, he remembered everything. He didn't want to believe what he had seen. It was clear to him, though; he knew it wasn't just some terrible dream but a vision. Ashley was trapped in darkness. The terrifying figure who'd taken her away was holding her prisoner.

Josep looked around at the expanse. He could see the horizon, far in the distance, beyond the white featureless void he sat in. There was nothing to look at in particular, so he stared at nothing. He hadn't noticed it before now, but it had been so long since he'd been alone that he didn't know what to do with himself. His tears had dried on his face after he blacked out. He thought to wipe them away but sat transfixed. There was no sun overhead, just a constant, sterile light all around. There was no way to tell how much time went by. Josep sat trying to come up with the right words. Something to convince the voice with. As he went to speak, he could feel he had strained his voice earlier. He cleared his throat to make sure his voice could be heard. "Hello?"

A moment of silence passed before the response came from behind again, "Yes, Josep. I'm here."

All the planning didn't mean a thing in the end. Josep didn't know what to say. "So what happens now?"

"Now you can rest."

Josep felt a cool blast of wind at his back. He tensed at the surprise and then turned his head to see what had caused it. Roughly thirty feet away stood a shimmering, pearly gate. A rainbow of colors he could only imagine the names for danced up and down its metallic surface. An ethereal golden light shone through the bars far brighter than the blinding haze he was finally beginning to grow used to. He took it in without blinking and rose to his feet. The top of the gate towered above him, maybe twice or even three times his height. He then took notice of the walls the gate sat between. A solid mass of lavender cloud on either side stretched all the way to the horizon in a straight line. Smoky wisps crawled along the ground past his feet. The clouds themselves were shifting and changing shape like he remembered massive cloud banks used to on the coast before a storm, but the wall itself stood solid and unwavering. The colors of the wall changed as well; purples and pinks swirled and mixed in hypnotizing combinations. The air that had been stagnant and constant before had been replaced by the gust coming from behind the gate. The wind was cool on his skin and made his hair stand on end. He couldn't imagine the source, but he felt it was wild and majestic, and it stirred something in his soul that he couldn't fully comprehend.

He stood entranced for a few moments before he instinctively took a step forward. If he could hardly understand what he was seeing glimpses of here, what must it be like on the other side? He had closed half the distance when the voice spoke from behind him again, "Enter, Josep."

Josep snapped back to his senses. This wasn't right. He felt a longing to continue but refused to let himself. He realized that he had an arm already outstretched to touch and open the gate. He took a moment to steel himself and his fist closed in resolve. He spoke to himself under his breath, "No." Josep took a step back, away from the gate and the light.

The voice spoke again, "You've done well, Josep. You fought the good fight. You strived during your life to do what is good and just.

With a pure heart and righteous intentions, you pushed to the finish line. Now your trials can end if only you will let it."

Josep's spirit was defiant. He knew he had done good. Not his whole life, but for most of it. But Ashley did far more. She was the whole reason he was here. She was the example he tried to follow. This voice had missed something. If it was God, then he was wrong. He had to be. Josep refused to accept it. "This isn't right. This can't be right. I won't leave her."

"She isn't here, Josep."

"Then I won't go at all." He looked up at the gate as he backed farther away. "You brought us together. How could you ask me to abandon her?"

"There is no asking, Josep. These are the consequences of each of your own decisions. You had the choice your entire life. You chose to leave her behind through your own inaction."

Josep's jaw tensed as his eyes welled up. It was true. He couldn't deny that now. And the truth hurt more than he ever imagined it would. "I-I know. I'm sorry." His head dropped, and he closed his eyes to hold the tears in. His lip began to quiver. "I'm so sorry, Ashley." He wiped at the single tear that escaped his hold. He wasn't sure where to look; the sight of the gate called to his spirit and made it harder to pull away. He locked his eyes on his bare feet and tried to ignore the billowy, mauve tendrils drifting by. "I should've acted then." A flurry of moments raced through his mind. "So many times...but I'm taking action now. I can't let it end this way. It's my fault." He wasn't quivering anymore. His mind was made up. He turned away from the gate to face the endless expanse. "Let her take my place! If someone has to go, then let it be me."

The voice came on the breeze that was now at his back, "Josep—"

Josep interrupted. He had to make him see. "I can be her substitute! If someone has to be punished, then I'll take it for both of us! Just let her go free."

"That's not how it works, Josep," the voice spoke unchanging, constant in its tone as if it had done this a thousand times before. "Not just any can act as a substitute for sin. The wages of sin is death and separation. But no man can conquer death on his own. You are bound by the same laws as every other man and woman and child. Who are you to change what has been laid before the foundations of the world?"

Josep knew not to challenge the voice's authority, but he had to make him understand. "I-I'll do anything. I can't leave her behind. I won't. She was my whole life. How can I just let her go?"

He stood there, looking off into the distance. Time passed in silence. The breeze coming from behind was the only noise in the world.

"Josep, you do not understand," the voice spoke softly. "The life you lived before will seem as only the blink of an eye. You will live more fully and experience more widely the universe as you have never imagined it. The world lies ahead of you, Josep. You must let go of the past and look ahead to the future. This reward is not gained by all, for the way is narrow. Accept and be at peace."

Josep kept his back to the gate. He had to. The offer pulled at his spirit. He had never truly reflected on the reality of his life after death. In life, he had simply followed the example he had seen in his bride. But again, he was here without her. He couldn't go on without her. Not when she had been his guide for so long. He couldn't bring himself to resist, but he refused to give in. Josep stood with his back to the voice, unwavering, focused on the image of Ashley in his mind. He had to remember and focus on her—to stay strong. He refused to be separated from her forever. His silence was deafening, though. After all, what was he doing? He must seem mad to turn away the gift of eternal happiness for the sake of one woman. But if he backed down now, wouldn't he be making a mockery of the life they had lived together? Perhaps this was a test. It had to be. It was all a trick.

After a long time had passed, when Josep had all but given up hope, the voice spoke again, "You reject paradise?"

Josep's eyes widened.

The voice continued, "In the face of eternal bliss, you decline?"

Josep lifted his head to the sky, hope growing in his eyes. "Will it save her?"

"This alone is not enough. She is already separated from this place. You have seen where she is."

The images of his dream returned to him. His heart broke at the thought of her being in such a place all alone. With a tight jaw, he answered, "Yes."

"You would have to travel into that place yourself. As a man alone, you would have to face death itself, just to find her. And to return, you would need to do the same again."

The voice paused, waiting for his response, but there was no hesitation.

"Anything. I'll do whatever it takes if it means she'll be saved." Josep stood taller now, his fists clenched, his spirit ready.

"You would do this alone, Josep. There will be no coming back should you fail."

Another gust blew against his back, and Josep turned to face the gate. Somehow, he had already forgotten just how wondrous it was. For an instant, he felt he might go through again, but he quickly squelched that feeling.

"I understand. But I won't go without her. If this is the only way, I'll do it."

Silence hung in the air for a moment, the magical wind blew against his face and called to him, but he refused to answer. He had a goal now.

"So be it," the voice said. "Then it is through this gate you must pass." Josep turned around again to face the expanse, and a new way had appeared. A single door, like the door on his own home when he was alive, sat alone in the vast whiteness. It was plain and white with a brass handle. It stood another ten feet away. And it called to him.

"Ashley is through there?" Josep asked.

"Many things are through this way, Josep. Things you will not understand. Things men were not meant to see. Should you lose your way, you will never find your way back. But you must persevere if you begin. You will suffer more than you ever have before. Even so, you will have only a chance to succeed."

The severity of the matter grew in Josep's mind. His heart had already made the decision, and he would not falter. His mind was only now catching up, though, and it made his heart race.

The voice continued, "But yes, it is through this way that you must go to find her. Heed my words, though, Josep. Once you have begun this journey, there is no going back. Be certain before you make your choice."

Josep thought to take one last look at the gate behind him, but he feared that if he did, his confidence would waver again. He focused himself on the door ahead. "All right. I've made up my mind."

"So be it."

Immediately Josep felt another surge of air behind him, this time almost pulling him off his feet. In a moment, it was gone, though. He turned to look and saw the gate had been taken away, the endless white expanse replacing it again. He faced the new door in front of him. He had made his choice. His mind was made up. There was no going back now. He walked forward and grabbed the handle. He took a deep breath, then he entered.

FIVE

As soon as he went through the door, things were different. The blinding white he was slowly growing accustomed to had vanished. He found himself in a hallway, roughly forty feet long. There were doors lining both sides and one at the far end. Fluorescent lights ran down the length of the ceiling. Compared to the white expanse, it was nearly pitch-black, but his eyes adjusted in an instant. Suddenly, he felt like he was alive again. Sensations weren't as vibrant as before, but he took more notice of them. He noticed his clothes as well and his body. He hadn't noticed before, or rather he didn't care enough to notice, but he was young again. When he had died, he was nearly a hundred years old and had grown used to the debilitating effects of a long life. Now he felt strong and young. How young he couldn't tell, but he felt like he was in the prime of his life. He was wearing jeans and a plain white shirt. He was standing barefoot on smooth, white tile. *Was I dressed like this the entire time? What…what was I wearing? It was just a moment ago, but it feels like it's been so long.*

Suddenly it was so hard to remember anything that had happened. It felt like entering another world just by passing through one doorway. But then again, maybe it was exactly like entering another world. He was alone now. Before, he could feel a presence surrounding him. When he spoke to a voice he couldn't see, it felt natural; he could tell someone was there. Now he could feel their absence. He was on his own. Where to go though? He hadn't thought to ask specifics before. Honestly, he was afraid if he waited any longer—if he looked at the gate any more—that he would be pulled in by its allure. Now that he was far away from it, however, he realized just how little he knew about where he was and what he was facing. Just to see, he spun around, turned the handle, and pushed on the door he just came through. He may as well have been pushing on a wall. It didn't really matter. He wasn't going back even if he could, but he couldn't tell if knowing he was trapped on this path filled him with determination or dread.

"It's all right," he spoke aloud to himself. "You've got this."

He faced down the hall to weigh his options. There were three doors on each side and one at the far end. There wasn't any visible difference between any of them. He walked forward to try the first door on his right, but after only a few steps, there was a massive thud against the second door on the left. Josep yelped in a panic. Another boom against the door, like someone—or something—was trying to break through. The door didn't shake in the slightest. It held firm. But the siege was relentless. An erratic, downright manic barrage of poundings continued. The sounds were muffled but powerful. Along with the banging were muffled roars.

Josep couldn't imagine what sort of thing would or even could make noises like what he was hearing. He found himself plastered flat against the wall as if that would somehow protect him if something did emerge from the door. After a few moments of panic, he continued toward the door on his right. However, this new choir of muffled violence he was listening to made him reconsider. Should he open any of these doors? What if they all housed some monstrous thing? He hadn't been on his quest for two minutes, and already he was wondering what he had gotten himself into. He weighed his options, but that only took a moment. He had very few choices.

There were six doors available, not including the door he had entered through. He glanced at the door that continued to shake with each attack that slammed into it as he thought to himself. *Well, obviously I'm not trying that door.* He looked around at his other options. *Actually, I'm not sure about any of these doors. Who knows what's behind any of them? For all I know, as soon as I open one up, some kind of monster...you know what? I don't wanna think about it. I need to test these things and just make my best guess. Ashley's waiting for me. Somewhere.*

The beast behind the door continued as he walked to the first door on the right. Once he approached the door, Josep noticed a strange vertical row of symbols etched into its surface. He didn't recognize them in the slightest. A column of four characters was evenly spaced. He was no linguist and couldn't even begin to guess what these might mean. They were simple in their design but gave no indication as to what they might mean. It dawned on him that they may not even be human in origin. He was beyond anything he should be able to comprehend. The familiar design of the hallway was bizarre in and of itself. He tried to guess as to what they might mean but quickly gave up the pointless effort. There was nothing else on or around the door to indicate what might lie beyond, so without any other options, and still too nervous to open it outright, he gingerly placed his ear against the door. He waited a few moments, still with one eye on the pounding door across from him. After a few moments, he heard a very small sound. It was somewhat quiet but distinct. A single clink. Like metal on metal. Another few moments, and another clink. It was rhythmic. Not mechanical, but continuous. It sounded like coins falling, one after another, but he couldn't be sure. He had precious little information available to him and far too much at stake to feel confident he could enter based on that alone.

He pulled away after another minute or so without a change to the rhythmic clinking. All the while the muffled roaring and pounding never ceased. He walked directly across the hall to test the opposite door. This one also had strange runes engraved in its center. They were different but gave no indication as to their meaning. He pressed his ear against this door and waited. This time, he heard right away a gentle weeping. Someone was crying softly. Not a panicked, anguished cry, but a slow, deep cry. Like someone who had felt sadness for a long, long time. He waited but heard nothing else. He moved down the hall, sticking to the wall across from the door with the feral thrashing sounds.

At first, he thought the noise began because of his entering the hall. Now he wasn't so sure. For all he knew, this creature had no clue he was even there. Whatever was behind that door was simply angry. A pure, unfiltered rage without a target. He made his way to the door across from the beast, pressed his ear against it, and then plugged his other ear to try and focus. It took a moment, but he finally distinguished a new noise beyond this door. A woman moaning. No, multiple women. A crowd of women all moaning like they were in ecstasy. He thought there would be some cause he could determine, but it was just as ceaseless as the raging across the hall. A cacophony of moaning from what he could only assume was some kind of orgy. Confused and feeling a bit guilty, he pulled away and continued to the last door on the right. Before he could even get close enough to press his ear against this door, though, he heard the noise beyond. Scratching. A skittering, clawing against the other side of the door. A host of hands or claws digging at the door. It wasn't forceful like a creature trying to dig through. It was slow and methodical, like a ballet on the wood. Whatever it was, it sent shivers down his spine, and Josep moved away quickly to the door across from it. He approached the last door, but when Josep pressed his ear against it, he heard nothing at all. A long, large endless silence. It wasn't that there was no noise beyond the door. The noise was the silence. It filled his ear and his mind and made him imagine all sorts of things. None of which made sense, truly, but all of which could lie beyond.

What am I doing? He wondered to himself, *I've just begun, and already I'm stuck. I can't even bring myself to open a door. It shouldn't be this hard, should it?*

The words echoed in his mind. He felt they were right, but somehow, they didn't feel like his.

I had perfect peace right in front of me, and I turned it away. I should just stop now before things get any worse. Maybe if I wait here for a while, the way back will open, and I can rethink this whole situation. I should just end it, here and now.

For a brief moment, he agreed. What fool would throw paradise away when it's within their grasp? His eyes snapped open, and he jerked his head away from the door. Guilt swelled up in his chest. How could he even pretend to entertain the idea of quitting on Ashley? She was his everything.

He then noticed his ear felt tender, and there was a bit of sweat on it as if he had been pushing it against the wood far longer than he realized. Immediately, he resigned to never approach this door again either. He looked back down the hall he had come from and didn't like any of his options. There was nowhere else to go; he had to choose one, but he would take his time in doing so. He paced up and down for a while weighing his options. He tested the first, second, and third doors again a number of times. None of the noises behind any door gave any indications that they had or would ever change or let up. The raging and pounding continued all the while, echoing in his mind. The sounds slowly filled him with anxious tension. He didn't want to choose any of the doors, but Ashley was waiting for him, and he had to go at some point.

For a moment, he decided to go through the third door, the one with the sounds of moaning. He told himself he was hoping it would be somehow pleasant on the other side, but he stopped himself short. He knew that wasn't really why his instincts had drawn him toward it. He felt another pang of guilt and wouldn't allow himself to choose that way. He now stood between the first two doors. As he weighed his options and tried to force a decision, he noticed that the door he had come through also had strange symbols engraved on it. They were small and unobtrusive, but somehow, he imagined, important.

After weighing his options for far longer than he would've been proud to admit, he settled on trying the door with the weeping first. He hoped whatever lay on the other side would be as sheepish and defeated as the sound suggested to him. He approached the door, grabbed the handle, and readied himself. He turned the handle and cracked the door open slowly, just enough to peek inside. It was a very small room. It was still white and sterile like everywhere else he had been so far, but there was a design on the walls, floor, and even ceiling. A grid of large squares all around made the room somewhat dizzying to look into at first. He continued to slowly crack open the door until he saw something on the floor near the back corner of the room. Someone was lying curled up, facing away from the door. It was naked and pale and shaking with each cry. It was this thing that was softly weeping. The door had muffled the sound of its crying, but it was still very tender even now. Whatever this thing was, they were very small and very frail looking. It was hairless and emaciated and hugging itself as it cried. Josep stood like a statue waiting for any sign of danger at all, ready to slam the door shut at a moment's notice. After a few moments without change, though, he readied himself before braving a word, "Hello?"

There was no change. The thing continued to weep to itself without acknowledging the intruder at all. Josep took a glance behind him at the rest of the hall. Nothing had changed out there either. The ceaseless rage continued unabated. He looked back inside, and the thing hadn't moved. He dared another attempt, "Hello?"

This time, the thing answered very softly, "What do you want?" Its voice was raspy and thin like it hadn't spoken a word in ages.

Josep answered, still holding the handle tight ready to retreat, "Who are you?"

The thing spoke between weeping, "What does it matter?"

Josep was taken aback by the question. He hadn't expected any sanity beyond any of the doors after what he had been listening to for what must've been hours now, much less did he expect questions in response to his own. The thing didn't move from its corner, so Josep took a small step to peer around the door and confirm it was alone. Josep couldn't tell from looking, but his foot sunk into the floor more than he expected. It was firm but pliable, like some sort of cushion. What he had mistaken for a painted grid were the outlines of dozens of pads that lined the surfaces of the room. It was like some prison or asylum cell, only without bars or locks that he could see. Still not trusting his audience, Josep spoke again, "I'm looking for someone. I was wondering if you could help me."

The thing responded, sniffling to clear its voice, "No. I can't. No one can."

"What do you mean 'no one can'? Why not?" With each answer, Josep's curiosity and confusion grew.

Still facing the wall, the thing mumbled a response, but the roars from down the hall drowned it out. Josep hesitated a moment but was committed to his choice, at least for the moment. He released his grip on the door that he had stepped past at this point, and it slowly closed on its own. As soon as it did, the roars disappeared, and there was nothing but the sound of his own breathing and the whimpering of the thing that lay at his feet. Josep nervously asked, "What was that?"

The creature whimpered for a few moments before responding, "Just go away. It doesn't matter anyways."

"It does matter," Josep said. "I've never done anything more important in my life. I have to find her."

The creature didn't respond. It continued to cry to itself and shudder as it did.

Josep asked, "Why are you crying?"

At this, the thing paused. It sniffled a bit more, then answered, "You used to cry too, didn't you?"

Confused, Josep hazarded a response, "Well, yes. Everyone does at some point. There's usually a reason, though, isn't there?"

"There's always a reason to. There's never a reason to stop. You would be crying too if you knew what I know."

Questions were brewing, but one came to Josep's tongue first, "What's your name?"

The thing curled up and hugged itself tighter than before, "Why does that matter? It won't change anything."

"I suppose it won't, but it would help me talk to you better." Josep shifted his stance a bit.

The creature shifted too; it began to look over its shoulder at Josep but stopped short as if it lost its nerve. "We used to know each other quite well before you met her."

Josep's eyes widened. "You know Ashley?"

The creature lay still.

"Who are you?" Josep insisted.

A moment of silence passed. The creature let out a sigh and began to move. With as little effort as possible and still tightly curled up, it rolled itself over to face Josep. It was just as pale and sickly in its face as could be expected. Its pale eyes were sunken, its cheeks were stained with rivers of tears, and deep wrinkles outlined its gloomy expression. Josep's eyes locked with the creature's, and for a moment, he felt a flash of familiarity. Josep's own mood felt like it sank in response to his host's; the only word he could use to describe the thing was pathetic. They sat and stared at each other for a few seconds before the creature built up enough energy to speak again, "My name is Despair."

Josep didn't know how to respond. He was dead now; he knew that. Somewhere in his mind, he expected to see things he didn't understand, but he hadn't expected this. Despair apparently could see the thought on Josep's face and so answered before Josep could ask, "Don't ask anymore, please. Just…if you want to go, then just go."

Despair began to turn away again, but Josep stammered to stop him, "I don't know where, though! Please. How do you know Ashley?"

Despair settled again, seeing Josep wasn't leaving. "I left you when you met her. Remember?"

Josep was struggling to comprehend what he was being told but wanted to keep Despair's attention without him turning away and refusing help. He thought for a moment, then spoke, "That was a dark time for me."

"It was all a dark time, Josep," Despair spoke like an old friend after a long time away. "It still is. It always is." His gaze drifted down, and it looked like he would begin to cry again.

Josep interjected, "It was…until I met Ashley. She changed everything for me. The rest of my life was nothing like it had been. I would have never ended up in heaven in the first place if it wasn't for her."

Staring at the floor now, Despair answered, "Is that going well?"

"It's not like that. I was in heaven, but for some reason, she wasn't. That's why I have to find her. I need to save her and bring her back with me." Josep was sitting on the padded floor now.

"Why?"

Josep was taken aback by such an alien question. It took him a moment to find the words. "Because…because she doesn't deserve to be here. She was perfect. Everyone knew it. She was the light that lit up my life—everybody's life! Every moment she spent helping others and encouraging them and taking care of them."

Despair interrupted, "And then she died."

Josep felt like he'd been slapped in the face again.

Despair continued, "She died. And you died. And all those people she helped will die. And they'll all end up here, and none of it will have mattered. It never does."

Josep was defiant, "No. No, it did matter. She made everyone's lives better. Our kids know that. Our friends knew that. Everyone did! That will last forever."

"No, it won't." Despair was still staring at the floor. Without an ounce of enthusiasm, he continued to tear everything Josep believed in to shreds. "None of that lasts. Your friends already forgot about half of the things Ashley did for them. If it takes a year or five—even if it takes a hundred, they'll forget it all. When they're dead, there will be no one on Earth who remembers any of it. Her name will sit on a rock for a few hundred years more, and then it too will fade away to nothing. Just like the billions who came before her, and the billions that will come after." Despair looked back up at Josep. "Did you know she was buried next to a man named Simon Keffler?"

Josep's growing indignation was replaced with confusion. "Who?"

Despair stared into Josep's eyes. "Simon Keffler was a husband and a father. He lived fifteen miles from you and Ashley's house. During his life, he kidnapped, raped, and killed nine girls and two boys, all of them younger than eleven. He abused his wife and daughter for years. Eventually, he died peacefully in his bed at the age of sixty-eight. Now he's here."

Josep's eyes filled with a spark of rage.

"And so is your wife. They both live here as equals now, and nothing she did ever mattered."

"Shut up!" Josep couldn't hold his tongue any longer. "That's not true. It did matter! It all mattered! So what if some monster was buried next to her? The difference is he deserved it! It's because of her I ended up in heaven. What else could matter more than saving the people she cared about?"

Without missing a beat, Despair answered like he was three steps ahead of Josep, "And yet, here you are."

Josep stuttered, "T-that's not the same. I'm not stuck here like he is or anyone else, and neither is Ashley! That's why I've got to find her and get her out of here. I've got to save her! She didn't deserve this. It was just a mistake."

"She can't be saved, Josep." Despair's gaze fell back to the floor. "No one can be."

"You're wrong. I can save her! I was already at the gates of heaven!"

Despair interrupted Josep again, "And what good did that do? You're still here. You're no better off than anyone else because of it. Even if you did find her, it still wouldn't matter. You're stuck here forever just like everyone else here. What's the point, Josep? Why bother?"

For a moment, Josep's spirit wavered. What was the point? How could he hope to escape this place without any help? He had no idea where to find her and could barely stand to even speak to the first person he'd met in this place. He refused to surrender, though. "I've seen heaven. I know we can get there. The voice I heard out of heaven told me that I could save her, and we could both make it back. I don't know how, but…we'll make it out. Together."

The slight hint of enthusiasm that made Despair engage Josep the way he did was waning. His eyes began to droop as he answered, "I've heard that before."

"What do you mean?" Josep shot back. "More people have come through here?"

Despair's eyes were nearly closed. "You're not special, Josep." His face began to tense up as tears welled in his eyes again. "No one is. No matter what you do, it'll just keep happening over and over."

Josep thought for a moment before answering, "I don't care how many people have failed. All it takes is one person to succeed to prove you wrong. I have faith."

Despair looked up quickly at Josep again before asking slowly, "In what, Josep?" His eyes were begging for an answer.

Josep almost shot back immediately but sank into those eyes. Somehow, Josep could see a million answers swirling within. Countless ways to say what he wanted to were lost in a sea of hopelessness. This wasn't right. It was all wrong, Josep knew that. But what more could he say? He had seen the gates of heaven himself, but what good was that now if he couldn't share that sight with another? What hope could fill such a gaping abyss of despair? Further words escaped Josep. He nearly thought he would succumb. Truly, what was the point of any of it? What chance did he have of facing the depths of darkness when entering a door to the unknown took him hours of dedicated effort and soaked his spirit in fear? Had the memory of his soul mate's face not been so fresh in his mind he might have even given up right there. But he couldn't. He wouldn't. There was a reason to it all. It did matter. His purpose was clear in his mind now. Her face called to him, longing for rescue. He realized then that he had been slouching now for a while, his countenance falling with his spirits. He straightened himself before standing. His voice was stronger now as well, "I know why I'm here, and I won't give up. I'll save Ashley no matter what. I won't let you convince me otherwise." He turned toward the door.

"It won't last. It'll end in tears. It always does." Despair was steadfast as he always would be. He rolled over—his back now toward Josep again.

Josep paused, feeling a great swell of pity for the creature. A piece of him wanted to stay to somehow save this thing. There were no words he could think of that would change his mind, though. As he prepared to leave, Josep spoke his parting words, "Not if I can help it."

Before Despair could drag his claim down again, he quickly turned the knob and stepped outside.

SIX

B efore he realized what had happened, he was outside. The door almost seemed to kick him out by itself. Josep was not in the hallway he expected. This place was new and very unlike what he was familiar with. The first thing that hit him, very literally it seemed, was the thick, heavy smell of sulfur. The heat was intense and weighed on him with every moment. The plain white door he left was now standing in a new kind of void. There was a distant but strong noise he couldn't identify that seemed to come from everywhere. The ground was a charred, gray stone, jagged and uninviting.

Josep stood on a platform about fifty yards in diameter. He couldn't see what was below, but there were flecks of ash floating up from the gap. The sky was an inky black. The only light was from below, and there was nothing to see in the distance. It was as if he was floating in a dark and empty night sky. There was a sort of path leading straight ahead to a massive structure that resembled a coliseum. The structure was far darker and seemed to shimmer against the dull orange glow from below. The shadows jerked back and forth in a most manic way. He immediately tried for the door again, but the handle wouldn't budge, and it was obvious there would be no going back. He stared at the plain white door—the last pure color he thought he would see for some time—to try and ready himself. He went to take a deep breath and calm his now-rapid heartbeat but choked on the acidic gas that filled his lungs. He had dealt with smoke before, and it didn't take long for it to cloud the senses, but this was different. If anything, his senses felt heightened now. Every fluctuation in heat on his skin was like a droplet rippling in a pool. Every sting in his throat was distinct and poignant and lasting. His eyes burned, and it was only in this reeling that he noticed the lack of any sort of wind. He took great notice of it in fact; the vacuum around him was perfectly deadly still.

He stood there doubled over and hacking for some time. He had hoped that he would grow somewhat accustomed to it with time; he did not. There was something in the gas that kept him fresh and alert to every sensation. When it became clear that this was not going to end, he resigned to push ahead. He pulled up his shirt to use as a makeshift mask, pressed tight against his mouth and nose. *I can't breathe!* He thought to himself as he struggled to stifle his panic, *I can't stay in this air. I've got to get away from these fumes before I choke to death.*

For a moment, he wondered if he even could die here. He didn't have the clarity of mind to worry about that right now, though. He desperately wanted a reprieve from the gasses that were filling his lungs. There was nowhere to proceed aside from the path that led toward the dark structure so he started toward it. When he began to approach the end of the platform, he realized the path was, in fact, a bridge. He went to the edge, and as he did, the sight that met him was hard to process. He had identified the origin of the sound he had been hearing. He squinted hard against the bright, fiery light below. His eyes widened instinctively but snapped closed quickly as they fought against the atmosphere. He was looking at a fall of immeasurable height. It appeared as if the entire world was in a massive well. At the bottom of the well was a monstrous, fiery pit, the cinders of which ascended all the way to where he stood. He couldn't lean far over the edge—even if he'd wanted to—as the heat was far more intense without the ground shielding him. The sound too was incredible even from what seemed like miles away the howl of the fire reached strongly up to where he stood, providing a horrific white noise. When he looked at the shape of the ground he stood on, it seemed like a titanic and twisted tree of dark stone growing up out of the pit. Where he stood seemed to be one of the loftier branches, though he couldn't see well enough into the darkness above to make out what might lie higher up.

The path he had before him reached toward the main trunk, and the whole of the tree spiraled in a gnarled fashion every which way as it led down. He was in awe until the disgust set in. What he hadn't noticed at first, but now couldn't ignore, were the people. They were only silhouettes against the blinding roar of the flames, but a constant, countless stream of bodies fell into the well everywhere he looked. Trying to make sense of the madness, he saw many throwing themselves from every branch of the tree while others seemed to be falling from the darkness above. Then his mind processed better the white noise he had been listening to. Screams. All around him, mixed perfectly with the roar of the fire was a choir of pain and terror. He hadn't noticed before, but now that he had identified it, his mind couldn't let go. Now the only sound he could hear were cries of anguish and rage far in the distance. He was already sick to his stomach from the fumes, but this was too much. He quickly turned away before he collapsed in sickness. His stomach was empty, but his body ignored that fact. He stayed there on his hands and knees for a few minutes. He would've been hyperventilating, but his body fought too hard against the foul stench. His body felt like it would give out at the slightest hint of surrender.

The chorus of torment echoed all around. This was hell. And Ashley was here. Somewhere. He wouldn't give up, he had said, and so he wouldn't. He wiped himself off before pulling his makeshift mask back over his face. At the first attempt to stand, his knees buckled and gave out. He hadn't realized how badly he was shaking. He wouldn't give up, but his second attempt was no better than his first.

He muttered to himself, "Get up. Get up, Josep. She's waiting for you. Get a grip! Move!" It was against every instinct in his body, but he finally managed to stand. He was still shaking, but he forced himself to turn toward the path and stumble forward.

"Focus. Just get through this and everything will be fine."

He focused on remembering the images he'd seen in his dream. He'd seen Ashley. She awoke in a cave and had been taken through a ruined city, and then some sort of prison, to a lone building among dark, swirling clouds.

He spoke the words to himself like a mantra, "I'm coming, Ashley."

There was no way to know if any of it was real or not. Right now, it didn't really matter. His goal was to keep himself distracted and move forward. He had to ignore the realities around him, or at least pretend to. It would've taken too long to try and comprehend the sights and sounds and smells. Time he didn't have. He did his best to focus on the way that lie ahead. Even so, it wasn't much more appealing.

The structure ahead was tall and foreboding. It also seemed, however, to be incomplete. The entrance was a simple gap in the wall at the end of the path. It didn't appear destroyed or dilapidated. For whatever reason, it seemed like it was designed to be unfinished. What seemed to be random chunks of the walls were missing. Abstract sculptures that lined the outside were asymmetrical and chaotically placed. Some stood on pedestals; others jutted partway out of the wall in random orientations. All of it, however, seemed to be made of the same shimmering black stone. Something akin to onyx or obsidian, though he would never know for sure if it was even from his world.

All the while, the uneven outline flashed with the dull glow of the flames far below. It took him some time to reach the entrance at the end of the bridge. By the time he approached, he realized it was much taller than he first thought. He was an insect in the face of a structure the world of his time could only dream of constructing. The chaotic architecture made him even dizzier to look at up close, almost as if its entire purpose was to confound and disorient. The entrance truly was a missing piece of the wall, no doorway or passage. The floor, however, was clearly delineated. Where he stood was jagged and rough stone. However, the ground inside was a very dark, fine sand. He took a tentative step forward, and for a few brief moments, he felt a sort of relief. His toes kneaded at the flour-like substance, and it was the first truly positive feeling thus far even if it was only a little thing. He relished the experience for a few moments before continuing.

The inside was truly like a coliseum. The sandy area was a large circular courtyard, devoid of any life or features. He scanned the perimeter and up and down the sides of the structure, trying his best to be as cautious as he could. He knew where he was now and knew how little he could predict with any confidence. He could only prepare so much, though, and continued to resolve in his mind that he had to push forward, no matter what. He saw a number of other gaps in the walls on the far side of the space that seemed, from this distance, to lead further beyond. He started toward no one in particular. The size of the arena was appropriately large for its height. The distance was maybe five hundred yards at a glance. Very quickly after distancing himself from the wall, he felt vulnerable. It wasn't just the similarities to a place of killing he stood in. It also wasn't the fact that he was the only figure out in the open in a place he knew was pure evil. More than he had ever felt in his life, he felt as if he was being watched. It almost felt as if he could literally feel the heat of eyes upon him. The paranoia was so strong he cried out at no one in particular, "Hello? Is someone there?"

However, there was no response at all. The choir of screams and the distant roar of the flames continued unabated, so he continued, looking over his shoulder every few steps. After minutes of walking, the heat continued until it became a physical pain; a single burning spot on his chest was slowly increasing in intensity. He had been diligently scouring every place he could for any signs of movement but hadn't noticed a thing. He tried briefly to listen for any signs of life but knew he wouldn't notice any noises with the backdrop of screams that continued in the distance.

He finally had to stop and see if there was something wrong with his own body. He lifted up his shirt to inspect but saw no signs worth noting. He turned all around to see if there was anyone behind. When he did, he felt the heat change to his back. It truly was as if a beam of heat was focused on him as he moved. He didn't know what to do. He had precious few options. His shirt dulled the heat but only in a very minor way. He had no other tools at his disposal, and the only ways out were all on the other side. He bunched up his shirt where the heat was focused, trying his best to build some sort of protection, and continued. The heat continued to grow. It eventually did reach a peak; the heat intensified until it was a distinct pain, but no more than that.

He had the idea to swap between walking frontways and backward every minute or so to alleviate the burning in one spot. Constantly his eyes darted here and there. Anxiety was a reality he could do nothing about at this point, so he pushed it aside as best he could. Still, there was no movement. At times, he thought he spotted a figure or a shape that resembled a creature; but upon quick inspection, they were simply a particularly oddly shaped sculpture affixed to the walls all around. His paranoia was building to a fever pitch by the time he approached the other side. By this point, the softness of the ground had grown from a minor delight to an old friend. When he saw that the ground returned to the same hard jagged stone as it had been before, his heart sank. He was nearly fifty feet away when something did alert his senses.

One of the sculptures ten feet up and above the gap he had inadvertently chosen to walk toward gripped him more than the others. He froze in place. It was abstract but also purposeful. In an instant, it grew to resemble a man sitting down resting with his arms crossed, one elbow on his knee. It seemed to be made of the same reflective obsidian it sat upon, but what caught him the most was its expression. It had no eyes or mouth or even face as far as he could define, but it seemed somehow painfully bored in a way he couldn't quite explain. Anything was terrifying at this point, though, and so Josep was. Nothing happened at first, but Josep couldn't stand the heat on his chest for long. In a panic, he shouted, "Hey!"

Almost immediately and against all his wishful thinking that no one would answer, a voice did emanate from the statue, "What do you want?" The voice was just as disinterested sounding as it somehow appeared. The thing was hard to distinguish against the backdrop, but Josep guessed it to be roughly ten feet tall if it stood straight, perhaps more. The odd-looking limbs he labeled as arms and legs were massive and stocky. The thing that sat on its shoulders resembled a cow skull. There was no movement that came with the voice, and Josep felt for a moment he would run in terror, but the tone at which the voice spoke confused him more than anything. He expected, if he heard anything at all, to hear the growl of a beast or some monstrous shriek. Instead, this being sounded more like a student who was on hour three of a terribly dull lecture being asked if he had a pencil to share. "Stop making such a racket."

Josep didn't know how to react but, until threatened, decided to act as cordially as he could. "Uh, sorry." Moments passed in silence, but the heat on his chest urged him to action. "I, uh, are you making it hot?"

"Yes, that's me. Not something I do on purpose. Just my job." Suddenly, the image of a tired toll booth worker flashed in Josep's mind. One in particular, actually, that he hadn't thought of in ages.

"Do…uh…" Josep had many questions on his mind at the moment, most of which he was far too terrified to bring up to something he was sure was a threat, but couldn't bring himself to treat as such yet. First on his mind was the heat. The second was where to go next. "Do you know where I can find my wife?" It sounded silly in his mind, but in light of the surreal landscape he was standing in, he continued, "I think maybe she's been taken to a building, like a house, but in some clouds."

The thing gave an exasperated sigh of all things, long and dramatic, before it finally did move and point, rather flippantly, to the gap below where Josep had been walking toward. It was then that Josep noticed a flickering light past the gap. Just outside the coliseum was a single iron torch affixed to the wall emitting a strangely eerie pink light. Without any apparent reason, the light filled him with a sense of dread, but the creature spoke up and snapped Josep to attention, "You're going the right way. Just go wherever you feel like, and you'll probably be right." Then there was another movement. A very long, wiry tail slithered out from behind the statue and slowly wrapped itself around his waist.

It continued to do this as Josep watched, and the heat pressed another question, "Uh…what're you doing?"

Like a convenience store worker being asked what aisle the toilet paper was kept on, and following a huff, "I'm doing my job."

Josep paused a moment but quickly realized no further explanation was coming on its own. He pressed again, "What's your job?"

"I tell you where you're supposed to go. If I had anything better to do, trust me. I'd be doing that instead."

"What? Just me?" Josep asked.

More annoyed than before, it said, "No, not just you. Everyone. I tell everyone who asks where they're supposed to go."

The tail finally finished its journey after it had wrapped around the statue's torso six times. The sculpture spoke again, though only out of obligation, "So you don't ask me about it anymore: The heat is how I tell where you're supposed to go. It also, conveniently, makes you leave me alone which would be great right about now."

The explanation didn't clear much up for Josep, but as the creature's annoyance grew, he feared that it might turn to anger. Josep stammered toward the exit, "Th-thanks! Um."

Sure enough, the annoyance was growing. For a moment, the heat intensified greatly, and a slight glow lit up what Josep assumed must be the statue's eyes, much less politely this time. "Go away."

Josep heeded the instruction and left quickly. Once he had passed the threshold of the structure and broke the gaze of the statue, the heat dissipated quickly. It was replaced by a new pain, however. It took a few seconds to set in, but his feet hurt more than he'd anticipated just by leaving the sand. He looked down to inspect the soles of his feet but panicked at what he saw. His feet looked like they had been skinned or burned by contact with the powder without him realizing it; his raw flesh sat exposed to the elements. He fell to the ground as his realization of the pain only made it that much worse. In the excitement of the moment, his body had let him ignore it until he felt safer, but now his feet were screaming in agony. Looking back, he saw a trail following from where he left the sand. A few footprints of powder transitioned to an equal number of bloody tracks. He yelped in pain but instinctively stifled himself as much as he could for fear that his noise would anger the statue inside. Blowing on the wounds provided little relief.

"You idiot." He berated himself, "Of course, there's not gonna be anything positive here. How could you be so ignorant?"

Nursing himself as best he could, he looked at what lie ahead. It seemed like each gap in the structure's wall led to a different bridge, each leading to a different branch of the massive stone tower. The one he now sat whimpering on led to a stairway that spiraled farther down. He attempted once to try crawling but stopped when his first motion pressed jagged stones into his knees. He hated everything about where he was but conceded that he'd have to sit there, suffering in the heat and the fumes and the screams with no progress for at least a little while.

"Great job, Josep."

His jaw was tense as he fought against the pain. Without anything else to do, he was squeezing his legs and muttering as he tried to distract himself. "Oh! This sand is so soft. It's like baby powder. Wow, so comfy! Moron."

He tried not to, but he looked around once more. His attempt at humor was swallowed up by the gloom around him. In life, he'd always used humor to try and lighten dark moods. Here, though, that wasn't an option. He knew in life if something like this happened, Ashley would be nervously tending to his wounds as he sat cracking jokes. He would laugh and make her laugh in spite of her concern, and despite the pain, he wouldn't trade it for anything. There were no laughs in this place. Only screams of anguish. He could barely breathe even with his shirt covering his mouth and nose. Time passed as he sat in throbbing pain with no hope of aid. Alone with his thoughts and his searing wounds, just within range of the strange pink light of the torch.

SEVEN

He didn't know how much time had passed. He tried to move after what he gauged was an hour or so but was still in too much pain to walk. Fortunately, after his novice triage, he concluded that the burns were shallow enough they weren't serious. However, they would certainly limit his movement for some time. Even his rest was a battle, though; the surface he sat on had no good places to sit. Every few minutes, he shifted as much as he could, unable to find any lasting comfort.

During this forced mediation time, his anxiety lowered some-what as nothing new threatened his immediate safety. He realized at this point that even though he had been traveling for many hours since his quest began, to his surprise, he felt no hunger. He was fatigued to the point of exhaustion, and his body longed for real rest, but he craved no sustenance. What really began to drive him mad was the thirst. His cotton mouth was accelerated by the noxious fumes he continued to fight against. He toyed with the beads of sweat that happen to run over his lips. They provided no relief but let him imagine the feel of actual water. This entertainment didn't last, however, and without anything to occupy his time, he finally took to attempting prayer. He felt sort of silly at first. He had been in God's physical presence earlier, after all, and knew he had been told not to expect any help. He talked to the void for a number of hours. He asked for help in a dozen ways. He asked for Ashley's safe rescue. He asked for healing to his body. In spite of this, not surprisingly, nothing happened. After some time, he stopped praying and transitioned to monologuing which in turn transformed into reminiscing. Moments when he could have spoken up drifted through his mind and filled him with regret.

"Why didn't you just tell her before, Josep? It would have been so much easier. You thought it was uncomfortable then, just look where you are now. What I wouldn't give to be able to go back in time." He let out a sigh. "And hinting around at it apparently didn't count. No, you knew it didn't. You just pretended it did so you wouldn't have to put the work in. I just couldn't bring myself to push it and risk hurting her feelings."

He paused again but tried to keep talking to distract himself from the screams echoing around him. "I can't believe something so small mattered so much, though. I mean, sure I knew it was wrong of her to be so…I don't know…exclusive? She was never cold. Like, she never turned anyone away. She could just be…self-righteous, I guess. Everyone needed to do this one specific thing this one specific way, or it wasn't good enough. But I never thought it would end her up here. She did everything else right: church every week, Bible study, raising our kids right, everything. I don't get how she could end up here and not me."

His ears latched on to a woman's voice in the choir of screams. It wasn't Ashley's, but it made him imagine what she was suffering at that moment. He swallowed hard, "I'm not letting her stay here forever, though. I'll right both our wrongs. I'll get you out of here, Ashley."

He didn't realize when it happened and had no way to tell just how long it had truly been, but at some point, he realized he could finally walk. It was by no means comfortable. He moved like he had returned to being the old man he'd grown used to over the years. He could continue, however, so he did. Ever so slowly and wincing with every step, he set himself back on the path forward wherever that was leading him. The statue had said whatever way he chose would probably be the right one, whatever that meant. With its carefree attitude, Josep doubted anything it said could be trusted in the least; but with no alternatives, he had resigned to improvising as he went.

The stairs he faced spiraled down farther than he anticipated. There was a sort of wall that enclosed the stairwell that seemed similar to the coliseum he had passed through. This new spire was very narrow, though, and provided little safety on the way down. Not trusting his stability in his current state, he made his way down very slowly, almost crawling step by grueling step. He could see down the gap the stairs circled all the way to the bottom or, rather, the lack of a bottom. From where he entered, there didn't seem to be an end as he could see the same raging, orange flames that lie at the base of the monstrous tree. He traveled this way for a while until it finally did, thankfully, end. The stairs just stopped at a drop-off that led down to the fire. Just before that, however, another gap in the wall revealed a new bridge.

At the end of this new bridge, he saw the gaping entrance to a very dark cave. The surface of this bridge was the same dark stone as before but seemed to have been traveled more or was at least refined to be much smoother than what he had dealt with up until now. It was by no means comfortable, but Josep welcomed any improvement, however small. His feet at this point had scabbed over a bit and still protested at every movement but allowed him to at least hobble forward. At the mouth of the cave, what struck him right away was the temperature change. Up to this point, every inch of his travel in this place had been like a forge—hot and driving and miserable. Even as he approached the cave, though, he felt a cool atmosphere. There was no wind, mind you. The air was just as stagnant and stale as it had been everywhere else, but it was cool and soothing. Without hesitation, he moved past the mouth and stood in the darkness. As he did, an image from his vision flashed in his mind. The space inside the cave looked very much like the cave he had seen Ashley in before she was taken away. The thought he was on the right track sparked a flicker of hope in his spirit, despite the foreboding darkness he was entering. Josep squinted as he peered into the cave. He couldn't see much yet, but he felt sure it was the same place he had seen in his dream. He spoke aloud the mantra he'd been chanting in his mind, "I'm coming, Ashley!"

As the words left his mouth, they echoed far more than he expected; the darkness magnified his voice so it seemed like he was shouting. He froze for a moment, hoping nothing would respond. When nothing did, he whispered much softer and to himself, "But I'm gonna do it quietly."

The light from outside cast dim shadows, but his eyes needed some time to adjust before he could even make out vague shapes in the darkness. The fumes were lessened too. For the first time, he didn't have to cover his mouth just to breathe. By comparison, this was an overwhelming respite from the agony outside. At first, there was nothing of note; but as his eyes slowly adjusted, he spotted a light inside what he now identified as a tunnel. The light was not an exit but a single sconce that cast a peculiar green light. He knew not to trust anything and kept his guard up best he could, but he'd given up resisting out of fear and started forward right away.

The walls and floor were even smoother now than they were on the bridge outside. It seemed someone, or something, had intentionally made this way far more inviting than any way he'd seen so far. As he moved toward the light, he walked past a number of other passages that branched off in different directions. He tried to make out what might lie in each but couldn't see well enough to make any guesses. By the time he reached the verdant sconce, he'd passed over a dozen of these passages. He'd been moving as quietly as he could but detected no signs of life at any point.

In the strange green glow, he could now see the options before him; the path branched into four new tunnels, each just as featureless as the last. There was no light anywhere—nor was there any sound besides his breathing and the now nearly muted sounds of screaming and roaring fires from outside the cave. Apart from the fear of the unknown, the darkness stirred no apprehension in him. Josep grew up terrified of the dark until one day he decided to train this fear away. He'd spent years as a young man slowly unlearning the fear he'd resented so much during his youth. By the time his life ended, he'd grown a sort of fondness for the dark and would often sit outside in the dark of the night with his wife to talk and count stars. There was a certain mystique he felt most couldn't appreciate about the dark. In a strange way, he felt more comfortable now than he had in the horrific brightness he'd been in before. Here, everything was calm and peaceful. That didn't help him decide his next steps, however. What he did fear greatly was getting lost without any chance of rescue. There was no way outside of the cave without returning to the coliseum; he knew he had no other options but to continue deeper. Having to decide his own fate, though, made this far more upsetting. *This is a terrible idea.* He chastised himself for what he was about to do. *There's no way this goes well. This has to be the right way though. I know Ashley was here at some point. Just take a deep breath and get it over with, Josep. There has to be a way out further in, right?*

After extensive deliberation and ultimately resorting on nothing more than gut instinct, he chose a path and continued. The green glow was left behind right away, and he was left in honest oblivion. There was no adapting to be done. He simply ran his hands along the closest wall and slowly stumbled his way deeper inside. He'd learned how to solve a maze when he was a young child. His father taught him to choose a wall and stick to it. Never before had he been forced to use this technique, but now he was grateful for what seemed like such a trivial thing before. The tunnel curved sharply, and the light far behind him eventually did vanish for real. He had no clue how far he had gone nor how far the tunnel continued ahead. What he was continually thankful for, however, was the continued silence. There were no signs of movement or any sounds apart from what he made in the dead abyss he was wandering.

For the first few minutes, he felt all right, all things considered. He hadn't gone too far and was confident in his ability to backtrack should he hit a dead end. As his options continued to multiply, however, his confidence waned, and a serious fear began to set in. He couldn't die, could he? He was already dead, so he couldn't die again, surely. Perhaps that was even worse, though. He was somewhat familiar with death now. Wandering aimlessly in an endless, silent black became a more terrifying prospect the more likely it seemed. Until now, he had been perfectly quiet or as close to it as he could manage with his bumbling about. However, it had been quite some time now, and his fear of finding something strange was now sitting in the shadow of not finding anything at all. At a certain point, he decided to venture a very timid call into the dark, "Hello?"

Even while trying to keep his volume low, his voice carried far deeper than he meant it to. His lone cry became a choir of inquisition, bouncing all around him. He felt a pang of regret that he hadn't started with a simple whisper. His call did inform him that there were a number of other tunnels branching off from where he stood. He had been sidling along the wall on his right side for a good long while now without any confirmation it continued the same as it began. When his echoes had subsided, he paused to give any recipient a chance to respond. Much to his chagrin—and relief—there was none.

It was hard to be sure of anything without the use of his eyes, but there was nothing he could sense that indicated he was approaching any sort of end. He wasn't pleased with his success thus far, but he was committed to sticking with his strategy until he had a reason not to. He continued like this for hours. The tunnel twisted and turned in all directions multiple times. On a few occasions, he froze in panic, thinking he had heard movement in the distance. If there was anything there, it didn't seem to care about his presence. Certainly, it was just his mind playing tricks on him at this point. He never veered from the wall he now felt very familiar with. Should anything truly bad happen, he still felt sure enough that he could follow it back to the green light and try another way.

Then, catching him quite off guard, something did happen. His foot splashed in some liquid, and the sound echoed around him. He recoiled at the sudden change. Tentatively, he tested the ground ahead of him; and sure enough, it seemed like his tunnel ran straight into some kind of pool. He could tell it wasn't water. The liquid was warm and slightly viscous. However, it felt strangely inviting as it numbed the aching of his foot within seconds. He was hesitant to trust it, but the tunnel ramped down into the pool only very slightly for the first few feet. He slowly treaded until his feet were nearly submerged in the pleasant fluid. His feet had been crying out for rest, in spite of his initial triage, and he was so grateful for true relief he let out an audible sigh. He tried not to think what the fluid might really be or what might lurk in the deeper parts of the pool. At this moment, he tried to appreciate any kind of change to his routine.

After a few moments, he decided to take this opportunity to truly rest. His muscles were aching, and when he sat down at the edge of the pool, his feet marinating in the liquid, he realized just how long he must've been walking. As soon as he sat down, he collapsed entirely and laid prostrate on the smooth, cool stone. This moment wasn't so bad, in fact. His body leapt at the chance to rest, and before he knew what had happened, he was in a deep sleep.

The next thing he could remember, he heard a sound in the distance. His eyes snapped to attention, and it took him a moment to realize they had opened at all. He still lay in total darkness. He sat up to face the noise; apparently, there was a passage directly to his left on the other side of the place he had collapsed. Had he not been disturbed from his slumber, he could've stayed that way far longer. He felt rested enough, and when he went to move, he realized his feet felt nearly fully recovered. Actually, he felt very good. His aching had been numbed beyond recognition, and despite having slept on a solid stone bed, he felt no soreness or discomfort. This registered as strange to him but took a backseat to what now sounded like footsteps running in his direction. Whatever it was, it was moving very fast, each footstep cascading down the hallways.

He stood up quick and strained to see anything. He stayed perfectly still, hoping to stay undetected. The thing drew closer, and he could now hear a frantic huffing. Closer and louder, Josep was sure the thing would crash right into him. The thing was maybe twenty feet away when he slid to a stop. It sounded now like a man panting in a panic. If it was a man, he had been in a full sprint until he was completely drained. He didn't seem to notice Josep at all. After a few moments of loud breathing, it sounded like he was trying to muffle his voice, mostly unsuccessfully. His heaving was rapid and irregular. Soon after the sounds of whimpering began, stifled weeping filled the gaps between his gasps for air. Josep stood affixed to his wall, motionless, feeling the fluid from the pool running down the backs of his calves. The man's whimpering eventually turned into mutterings. He cursed under his breath and whispered to himself, "I just want out. I just want out of this place. Please, please, please. I wanna go back outside. God, let me out of here, please, please. Anywhere is better than here. I won't let it catch me again. Please, God, get me out of here."

Josep was reluctant to identify himself. But the man's quiet pleading continued earnestly and gripped at his heart. Josep was sure he knew the way out, or at least a way out. He tried to whisper as calmly as he could, "I know a way out."

Despite his attempt, the man panicked immediately. He yelped, and Josep could hear him begin to shuffle back the way he came along the floor.

"No, no! I'm a human! I'm not going to hurt you, I promise!" Josep stepped forward trying to calm the man though he was sure neither of them could see the other in the slightest.

"No! I'm not going back!" Despite the sheer terror Josep could hear in the man's tone, he kept his voice as low as he could manage. Even so, the man's panicked cries rang out and traveled far back into the unknown.

Josep continued, "I won't make you! I want to help! Listen, this wall leads back to the exit!"

The man showed no signs of trusting Josep's advice and continued to scramble away. It sounded like he was back on his feet. "Shut up! Just go away! Leave me alone!"

The thought of being alone again swelled up in Josep, and he yelled out, "Wait! Don't leave! I can—"

The man interrupted, "Shut up! You're too loud!" though he himself was just as loud at this point. Suddenly something pierced the darkness. It felt like a violent blade slicing Josep's vision after such a long time of being without light. Josep could now make out shapes and silhouettes in the tunnel. The pale blue light was flashing like static. He could see now the tunnels had grown taller and wider than they were at the start. When he began, they were a little above his head; now, he couldn't make out the ceiling at all. The hallway Josep was looking down ran straight ahead far into the darkness. There were far more branching paths now than he had realized. Every ten to fifteen feet, there was another way on each side of the passage. The light itself was coming from an adjoining hallway forty yards or so past the stranger.

Josep could see his outline now; the man was thin and disheveled. His skin seemed to reflect the light like he was covered in some kind of oil. Beyond that, Josep needed more light. As soon as this light began to flicker, the man's panic became abject horror. He abandoned any attempts at quieting himself or maintaining a level head. His voice was like that of a wild animal, shrieking into the void, "No! I'm not going back!"

He turned and ran toward Josep as fast as he could manage, and faster. He turned down Josep's hall and dashed into the black. Josep was frozen for a moment in shock, but only for a moment. He glanced back toward the light to see its source, which had now turned the corner. A massive, clawed hand pulled a female torso into view. Its body barely fit around the tight corner and filled every bit of the passageway. It crawled and shambled erratically like a deranged beast as it moved. Sitting atop the neck was the source of the light: a box that resembled a TV replaced the monster's head. The screen had a fuzzy blue snow on display, and the sound of TV static became the sound of doom.

Josep could just make out the shapes of cables running out the back of the set and back into the blackness. He took all this in in an instant and wasted no time scrambling to his left to follow the man as fast as his legs would carry him. After only a few steps, he realized that his feet had not recovered as much as he had assumed. He nearly stumbled to the ground but was determined to keep himself moving, and as he did, his feet screamed in protest with every step. Running in the pure dark only lasted a few seconds as the monstrous figure behind him rounded the corner and cast the flashing blue light against his back, illuminating a few feet in front of him. He caught glimpses of the man in front of him, arms flailing wildly. Josep would have screamed if he wasn't quite so terrified. The man in front of him screamed enough for them both, though, his howling truly sounding like some dying animal.

Josep's mind was racing but couldn't formulate any clear thought besides his need to flee. His silent journey through the tunnels for what could have been days as far as he knew was now very different. The pounding of the massive weight and the scraping of the nails on stone behind him flushed his body with adrenaline. Now he, too, was gasping for air and heaving as he ran. The one plan he had was to follow the wall on his left. The man in front seemed to be doing this as well until suddenly he turned sharply to his right and down another path.

"HEY!" Josep screamed to get the man's attention but was certain he couldn't hear him in the slightest. The man's raving drowned his voice out completely. Josep had only an instant to decide, but it only took him that long. He pitied the man but had his own survival to think about now. Josep continued the way he had come, keeping to the wall on his left. The thought flashed in his mind that maybe the creature would follow the man's terrified screaming and give him the chance to escape. It only took a few seconds for that hope to be dashed. Josep turned another corner, and, to his dismay, the light followed him instead.

The clawing and pounding of the creature were closer now too. The sound of static was bouncing off the cave walls and buzzing loud in his ears. Josep was slowed by his pain. The thing was much larger, too, and seemed to be just as eager to catch him as he was to leave it behind. Josep had no real way of knowing but thought if he could just keep up his pace a little while longer, he would make it back to the tunnels that were too small for the woman to pass through. This hope too was fading rapidly, though. With each stride his stamina waned, his breath grew heavier, and the sound of static grew louder. He turned one last corner and thought for sure he could see a faint green light far in the distance. A flash of relief sprouted within and just as quickly was destroyed. Before he could move toward the light any more, he jerked to a halt as the massive hand snatched him up. It gripped around his waist so tightly he thought he would be crushed. The monstrous hand picked him up with ease as if he was no more than a doll. The woman crouched up on her hind legs and held him aloft for a brief moment. He stared in horror at the massive screen. The flickering, blue light was blinding. This close, he could see the static playing on the TV far more clearly than he ever wanted. For a few moments, he thought he saw flashes of a face, of a woman or women. They were laughing, screaming, and crying. They were strangers but were somehow familiar. Before he could process anything, though—and with his mind still screaming to get away but without any chance of escape—the hand pulled him away from the screen before smashing him into it with all the force it could muster. The last thing Josep remembered was the sound of shattering glass, the roar of TV static, and the ghostly blue light from the screen.

EIGHT

"She's gonna love this, Josep."

Josep hit the breaks faster than he meant to. He'd forgotten where he was for a moment. "Wo! You okay?" Claire gripped the bags in her lap to keep them from falling.

"Yeah, yeah, sorry. I just spaced out there." He refocused his mind on his driving. "Sorry about that. You really think she'll like it?"

Claire returned to her usual perky self. "She's gonna love it, Josep, really. It's such a sweet idea too! Ashley's super lucky to have a guy like you who cares so much."

Josep was nervous. He had no apprehension at all; he was honestly giddy as a schoolgirl. He just wanted everything to be perfect. It had to be. She was. "You're sure Dan is going to make it out of work on time?"

56

"He better! I made him promise he'd be there to back you up." Clair was a petite girl, but far more feisty than her small frame would let on. Josep was glad she was in his corner for all this. "I think you may have overdone it a bit with the supplies. You might as well have just bought all the fireworks they had at this point." She chuckled. "I can't believe the guy at the store's reaction when you told him what it's for!" Her laughter was so full she turned the heads of two passersby outside her window.

Josep smirked. "Well, it's not my fault no one else goes all in for a proposal. They just don't have a girl as awesome as mine."

Claire mocked his sentiment with a faked gag. "Ew. So mushy. Ya know I never expected you of all people to be such a marshmallow. The first time Ashley introduced us to you, I thought for sure you would be all stoic with your tall, dark, and handsome vibe."

"Well, I don't mean to gross anyone out." Josep turned the car toward home. "I just love her is all. I wanna make it as special as I can."

Claire glanced at the row of bags filling the back seat. "Well, I think you already accomplished that. It's a good thing you have such a good-paying job, or you'd have to spend your future marriage living in an alley."

The word filled his stomach with butterflies. "You know she's gonna say yes, right?"

"Of course, she's gonna say yes, Josep. She's been dying waiting for you to ask for weeks now."

Josep had planned this out for more than just a few weeks. He'd rehearsed what he'd say, where everyone would be, the whole experience. He hadn't been nervous even the night before, but with each second that passed, he wondered if he'd be able to get the words out when the time came. "I just hope I don't screw it up."

"Honestly, you could just flash her the ring and give her one of these"—Claire raised and lowered her eyebrows in an exaggerated fashion—"and she'd lose it. Seriously, you're gonna do fine."

He had to do better than fine, though. Fine wasn't enough.

The sun was setting now. Claire had gone home and would be bringing Ashley any minute. Josep stood at the top of the hill overlooking the city. Dan showed up only a few minutes earlier but fortunately had enough time to set up below where the fireworks were ready to go. Josep's foot tapped feverishly as he went over his speech in his head again and again. There was a trail of rose petals that lead from the gazebo where he stood, down the path, and around the corner to the parking lot. He walked to and fro, dressed in the blue shirt and black vest Ashley loved so much. Candles lined the railing and as the sun dipped lower their effect grew stronger. The weather had held up like he'd hoped, and it seemed like everything was falling into place just right. The tension was swelling. The moment he'd been looking forward to for so long was now at hand. His heartbeat echoed in his ears as he paced back and forth. He heard a car pull up just out of view. He turned and stepped into position, making sure his tie was straight, and everything was put in place. He heard Claire and Ashley laugh and the door close. Josep had kept the entire thing a surprise, and Claire had sworn a vow of secrecy.

Now that he was here, he thought how she must know for sure what was happening; it was very strange that Claire would drop off her sister to meet him here of all places. He hoped it would still be something of a treat to be as prepared as he was. If nothing else, he had the fireworks to rely on. He heard a small gasp just out of view. She'd seen the start of the trail he'd laid out. He swallowed hard. He felt like he could float away or scream; he couldn't decide which. Then she appeared. His heart stopped. The world did with it. The sounds of the busy city in the distance faded into silence. She was glowing. She cast a light around her that drowned out all of the candles that were only a moment ago casting more and more shadows all around. The world was bright now like the sun had come up and brought a hundred more with it. He wasn't tapping his foot anymore, but he didn't notice. All he could see was her. She saw him and gasped again, her hands to her mouth. He held a hand out to her, inviting her closer. She floated along the path, the petals he'd laid out drifting on the magic wind that trailed behind her. She was like a goddess. By the time she entered the quiet shelter, her eyes were wet, and her face was flushed. He took her hand in his, and as he did, a chill traveled up his arm and through his whole being. He didn't deserve this. He didn't deserve her. He wasn't scared anymore; he was in awe.

"Ashley, I love you."

She held back her tears with her hand tight to her mouth. He stared deep into the universe that lie in her eyes. The few stars in the sky were outnumbered a thousand to one by the twinkling he saw there. He continued, "I know I don't deserve you, but I've loved you since the moment I saw you. For two years now as I've been allowed to be with you and know you, I've done nothing but loved you more and more with each passing day." He slowly fell to one knee, eyes locked with hers. "You've heard me say it a thousand times and ways, and if you'll let me, I'll say it ten thousand more. I'll never stop loving you. I promise to protect you, to care for you, and to never leave you for a moment no matter what this life might bring." He pulled out a small box and lifted it up. He opened the lid to display the dazzling jewel he'd been pocketing for weeks. "Ashley Bennett, if you'll have me, I swear this: There is nothing in heaven or earth that will ever pull me away from you in this life or the next. Will you marry me?" He spoke the words like he was born to. They came out without a thought in his mind, and he waited anxiously for what he could see was swelling in her eyes.

She choked back tears, determined to hold them in as long as she could. As soon as she could muster them, the words came, "Yes! Yes, of course, I will!"

He smiled ear to ear, his heart overwhelmed with joy and more than a little relief. He'd done it, and now his life would truly begin. A new life with the woman he'd been madly in love with since the instant he'd laid eyes on her. He slipped the ring onto her finger. As he did, right on cue, a loud pop sounded off to the side. Perfectly in view, fireworks began to light up the now darkened sky. It was perfect. The magic moment was complete. As she looked to her side in shock, watching the cavalcade of celebration fill the open sky, he gingerly took her hand and slipped the ring on her finger. He didn't know what to do with himself; he was elated. It was the happiest moment of his life.

Ashley looked back and locked eyes. "Now you'll be mine forever, right?"

Josep smiled. "I'll never leave you. I promise."

Ashley's smile grew wider. "You swear?"

Josep paused for an instant. "Of course, I do. Always."

Ashley's smile grew wider still. "You wouldn't leave me alone, would you?"

Something was wrong. For a moment, Josep was petrified that it was something he'd done. Ashley's smile stretched further still. Her face warped into something it shouldn't. "You wouldn't let anything happen to me?"

Josep froze. This wasn't right. This wasn't Ashley. It wasn't. This wasn't supposed to happen. The sky was very dark now. There were no stars. It was blacker than night, and the world began to fall away. Ashley's face had stretched so much he thought it would split into two. "You wouldn't go somewhere nice and leave me to suffer? Right, Josep?"

Josep's eyes were wide in horror. His angel was contorting before his eyes. He felt a hand grab his leg. He snapped to see what it was. Another arm leapt out from beyond the candles that warded off the blackness. A swarm of monstrous, clawed hands snatched at each of his limbs and pulled him back. Ashley had become something now. Her face cracked, and her angelic glow became an oppressive fiery flashing. Her calm, musical voice turned to scraping and biting to his ears. "You wouldn't leave me to suffer in a pit, would you, Josep?"

"No! No, this isn't—I didn't!" His mind was clearing or blurring back to the nightmare he'd been in. His perfect life was falling away to a void he couldn't reach. Tears of panic and horror streamed down his face. "I didn't mean to! I wouldn't!"

He clawed at the ground to stay in the past, where he had a chance, where she was. The thing that had been her was now a distant, taunting aberration. "You wouldn't send me to hell and save your own worthless soul, would you, love? I wasn't worth the trouble?! I deserved this torment?! You love me, right, Josep?!"

Josep screamed in horror at what he'd seen at what he had done. He was torn away by the hands into the blackness, into the void where there was no hope, back to where he was.

NINE

Josep woke in panic. He was screaming, or at least he was trying to. He could feel the fresh trails of tears down the length of his face. He instinctively went to wipe at them, but his arms couldn't move, or refused to. It was pitch-black. He felt very nearly like he was sleeping. It was warm, and the air was heavy and thick. He gasped for air but couldn't catch enough. He felt like he was suffocating. Not just his arms, his whole body refused to move. He felt numb. His eyelids drooped, and though his spirit cried out to keep them open, they fought back with every moment.

As his senses slowly returned, and his heart slowed, he heard a sound. Something heavy scraping against stone. It was all around him. Then he heard the rattling of chains in a rhythmic way. In a moment, he thought it sounded like someone dragging something with a chain. His body longed for sleep and pulled hard at his mind to comply, but he wouldn't. His body was very heavy when he could feel it at all.

The smell of something sweet and sickly filled his nose and mouth. He recognized the taste. It smelled like Ashley's perfume, a favorite she had worn for many years. The smell was comforting and soothing. His eyes fell shut again. The smell was happiness and comfort, and it filled him with a sense of peace and contentment. It was Ashley all around him. He gasped at the thought. He forced his eyes open. Ashley. He had to find Ashley. His body wouldn't listen. All he could muster was to bite at his cheek. As he pressed, the pain grew, and he managed to keep himself awake. Where was he? He had to find some way to move. He tried to move his head. Like a newborn, he felt he could barely manage to move at all. With all his might, he tried to throw his head forward. He only managed an inch or so, but it made him realize a few things.

He was lying on his back. His head landed on something soft that cushioned him. It felt like he was laying on her lap again. He felt like he was home. There was nowhere in the world he'd rather be. His eyelids faltered again. Every second was a battle that drew on every ounce of will he had. Slowly, as he fought back and forth against the tide of slumber that pulled at his mind, he began to realize more and more details, one at a time.

He was in some sort of box or coffin. The inside was lined with cushions that felt more perfect than any he'd experienced in his life. Everything drew his mind back to thoughts of Ashley. There was some kind of cloud inside with him. It filled every part of his prison, clouding his mind and numbing his senses. He had no sense of time. For a long time, he heard the sounds of his box being dragged across a stone floor, then suddenly, he was upright; and all was silent. He tried desperately to keep his wits about him or to summon them fully at all. At his best, he could swing one of his hands about for a few moments. His confinement was very tight, and there was no opening he could find.

Time passed this way. He dreamt dreams of his life, perfect moments replayed in his mind a thousand times. Each and every one ended in horror. Time and time again, he was stripped from his bliss in a ruthless fashion and thrown back into reality without mercy. He couldn't take this. To be so at peace only to realize he'd forgotten over and over how much pain he was truly in. Finally, it grew too much. In the moments he regained control, he mustered all of the pitiful strength he could and threw his head at the lid of his tomb. It was only a few inches in front of his face, but it was hard. The first time he tried, he collided with his nose instead of his head and felt for sure he'd broken it. The spike of pain was intense, and for a few moments, it helped him push through the fog that clouded his mind. Within seconds, it was back, though, and he continued to fall in and out of nightmarish dreams.

Every moment he was lucid, he used all his energy to lazily throw his head against the stone in front of him. It was torture, but he had no other options, and he refused to surrender. Again and again, in and out of reality. He'd watched his life back a hundred times by now. He must've, he thought. Eventually, and much to his surprise, there was a crack. A piece fell away in front of his face, and a very faint light shone in. Instantly, the fog began to stream out of the box; and as clear air slowly crept in, his mind whirled to life. He gasped desperately for real, honest air. What he could breathe now was musty and stale, but it was life and relief to him in that moment. He blinked hard and tensed every muscle he could feel trying to wake up.

Like a man coming out of anesthesia, his body returned to him in a slow, almost imperceivable wave. As he slowly came to, the faint green light he could see through the crack grew brighter. His recovery began to stall, and he longed for release all the more. Now with some of his strength returning to him, he continued to throw his head at the wall. The pain was more acute now as well. His head was throbbing like he'd never experienced. He thought he felt a drip of something fall from his eyebrow. His vision was blurry in the best of moments, but he refused to relent. Each attack revealed more light as small pieces gave way and fell out of view.

At long last, he had a small viewport in front of him, and his lungs were truly clear. The stronger he grew, the more he realized a few things. For one, the lid he was trying so desperately to remove wasn't solid stone as he'd thought. It was solid but fell away almost like it was made to be destroyed. Certain pieces fell away in chunks like they'd been held together by some sort of adhesive, like a vase that'd been glued back together after being broken. The other thing he noticed was that he was much weaker than he should've been. Even as he could feel his mind fully clear, his body was very drained. And the thirst. The thirst was almost too much to bear. Each breath he drew in felt like a brutal vortex across a wasteland. As much good as the clear air did him, he felt that much more desperate for relief from the thirst. This motivated him to fight harder. He slapped against the wall and kicked like a child in the meager inches of space he had to wind up. Eventually, though, the whole thing began to crumble; and then all at once, it gave way completely.

He didn't realize it had been supporting him in places, and as soon as it collapsed, so did he. He fell forward with no chance of catching himself and landed face-first on the cold stone floor. It was bone-chilling the moment he left the comforting confines he'd been in. He struggled with all his might to lift himself onto his elbows. In the dim light, he saw his arms, and it caught him off guard. He was very thin like he hadn't moved in a very long time. He then noticed his long hair dangling in his face and the beard he had grown. He had been there a very, very long time. When he realized just how long it must have been, a panic swelled up in him. How long had it been? Another drop of blood fell from his forehead and splashed on the floor. He went to touch where it had fallen from but ended up moving his head to his hand rather than the other way around. He felt a moistness but also a roughness. He prodded further and then snapped away at the sudden pain. His head was raw. It felt like it had scabbed over a dozen times and just recently been opened again. His head was pounding, and his body was aching. And the thirst. His mouth felt puffy and swollen. He tried to look around as best he could with his weak muscles.

He was in a small room no bigger than ten feet across. It was dark inside, but the green glow of a light came in through the open passageway. For a moment he noticed his breath forming ghostly clouds, and he realized how cold it was. He felt his toes curl as the cold stone floor began to bite at his exposed skin. He glanced behind to view where he'd been held for so long. It was a coffin or something like it. His was not the only one, though. The back of the room was lined with five similar boxes, each one a rectangular prison made of some kind of stone. Some had cracks like he could see in the surface of his; others were pristine.

As his gaze lowered, he turned away quickly at the sight of all the filth that was slowly flowing out of what had been his coffin. He finally took note of the stench and gagged. He tried to pull himself forward. He slowly crawled toward the doorway as he continued to regain what little strength he had left. When he made it to the wall by the door, he began to work his way to standing up. It was like learning to walk all over again. He fell a number of times, more than once all the way down, nearly hitting his face again. Every second was agony. How long had it truly been? He realized however long it was Ashley had been going on without him. He focused all his will. This thought was like a needle in his mind. However long it had been was too long. He had to get back on track.

He finally made it to his feet, gripping the corner of the doorway as best he could for support. A sudden realization snapped in his mind and set his senses on overdrive. He remembered the sound of his coffin being dragged along the floor and the image of the monstrous woman that caught him before flashed in his mind. He was in danger. He remembered where he had been for so long now. He had to be careful, or he risked being imprisoned again, or worse. There were no sounds he could make out. He dared a careful glance outside his room. A familiar sight greeted him. He was in a hallway, exactly like he had wandered before he was caught. The key difference was that now he had light. Whether this was an improvement or not was yet to be determined. Lining both sides of the hallway as far as he could see in both directions were sconces casting a pale, green light. Shadows danced all around as the small, oddly colored flames flickered in their places. He could just barely make out the ceiling about thirty feet up into the darkness. Every so often, as he had grown used to, there were branching pathways. A nearby doorway he could see led to a room much like the one he stood peeking from now. Neither way, to his left nor his right, revealed any signs of where they might lead. He was in a maze just as much as he had been the moment he entered the cave. It was so much colder now than it had been when he entered, though. At first, it was a refreshing respite from the abusive heat outside. Now it had grown so bitter his teeth chattered, and he shivered uncontrollably.

Somehow, he began to long for the sweltering heat once more. He listened closely for any signs of movement. The only thing he detected was the occasional crackle of one of the flames that lit his way. He finally dared to venture forth. His weakness forced him to move slowly, dragging himself along the wall. His once-white shirt was now ragged and stained. His jeans were soiled, and the thought of checking his condition underneath made him sick. He tried to move as quietly as he could, but the little control he had over his body now resulted in him slapping his feet against the stone floor every other step. The sound echoed for a distance around him and filled him with dread. He knew if anything caught him now, he'd be doomed. Each step slowly made him feel more like himself, but it would take some time before he could move like normal.

After following the wall until he came to a turn, he glanced as stealthily as he could. With one eye, he slowly slid the new way into view only to be greeted with another very long hallway exactly like the one he was in. Again, there was nothing in sight, and there were no signs of where to go. He had nothing to rely on but his old trick, and in his current condition, "hug the wall" was more than just an expression. He turned the corner and continued. Every few dozen yards, he came across another small chamber like the one he'd been held in. Each had a number of stone boxes lining the walls. Some were cracked like his; most were sealed tight. A few here and there caught his eye as they were wrapped tightly with chains.

He made his way to another hall on his right and stuck to it. After shuffling a bit more, he realized that if he took the next turn available, he would be going in a circle. Sure enough, after testing his theory, he ended up back where he started, his room the only one he'd found with a completely busted coffin. Now he felt truly lost. Every turn looked the same. Every hall lit evenly with the same pale green glow. Just then, something broke that monotony. At the far end of the hall he stood facing, a number of the torches suddenly changed color, the flames now casting a vibrant pink hue all around. Motion triggered his alarms, and he ducked back into his room as quickly as he could.

He peeked out from his hiding place just enough to make out what was happening. The silhouette of a woman was floating across the hall down another passage. Her curvaceous figure hovered backward and beckoned for someone to follow her lead. A few moments later, Josep gripped the wall tighter at what he saw. Some…thing was shambling behind the woman, captivated by her image. The bloated figure was hard to make out from this distance in the odd light. Its body was a bizarre shape as if it had tried to be something resembling a man at one point but failed. A massive hunk of flesh seemed to be attached between its legs and dragged on the floor behind it. It quietly moaned with what appeared to be its arms outstretched in front of it, pawing for the woman.

Like some sort of living dead, it was shuffling down the corridor, following the shadowy woman. The sight disgusted Josep and terrified him. But a thought occurred to him: *Would they lead the way out?* It sounded insane, but then again, nothing had been sane for some time now. After they had been gone nearly a minute, the sconces returned to their pale green glow, and the thought of being lost in the labyrinth spurred Josep onward. It took him some time, hurrying as he was, to reach the spot he had seen the pair appear. He cautiously looked around the corner and only saw a flash of pink for a moment before the light at the end of this new hall also returned to its usual green.

He hurried to keep track of the light, hoping beyond hope that it would lead somewhere new. This hallway was just a bit shorter than the one he'd just come from, and so it didn't take quite as long to reach the end. As he shuffled along, he kept glancing in the rooms and hallways he passed. They were all repeats: the halls lined with green light and the rooms all filled with coffins. Then his eye caught a different room. It was roughly the same size as the coffin chambers—small and square. This one had a pool of liquid that filled the room, however. It looked like oil with the glow of the green lights reflecting off its surface in odd ways. It was still, and there was nothing else in the room to identify what it might be for. He was curious but had to keep up the chase.

When he turned the next corner, he stopped quickly as he saw the shadow of the woman disappear into one of the rooms halfway down the passage, the beast in a slow but determined pursuit. Josep watched as it clambered into the room, moaning as it went. He heard quiet splashes and then silence. The lights around the room stayed pink for a few minutes before reverting to normal. The stillness remained as long as Josep waited. He was reluctant to draw any closer, but it grew more apparent that nothing was going to happen otherwise. He made his way down the hall until he came to the room they had entered. He quickly shot a look inside and saw it was just like the earlier room he'd seen with the pool. The dark liquid was reflecting the light and sitting still now. There were no signs of the creature nor the woman that Josep could see.

The room was small, there was nowhere else they could have gone inside. Josep remembered the mystery fluid he had rested his feet in. The memory hit him like a bygone era. The thoughts were blurry, but he remembered how soothing it felt. That softness felt familiar yet again to him. His coffin brought a very similar feeling of rest and relief, only to a horrifying extent. This was all interesting and piqued his curiosity, but it was no help to him as far as he could tell.

He was still very lost and had no guesses as to how to proceed. A shiver ran across his body. It was so cold now. His bare feet stung like needles whenever he felt them at all. He was tempted to step just an inch or two into the pool, hoping it would somehow be warm and ease the pain. The fear of something splashing out after him overpowered that urge, however, and he resigned to deal with it for now. He looked all around and pondered for a while. Eventually, he had to make a decision; it was either that or head back to his coffin in despair. He'd met that poor creature, though, and already promised himself he wouldn't end up like that. Every direction looked just as bad as the other to him. Then he had the idea that maybe the pair he'd followed ended here but began their journey at something like an entrance. Maybe that was his way out.

He traced his steps back to where he'd first seen them and headed in the direction they'd come from. Immediately, he was back to the maze. Every turn was the same. Every room was either a pool of liquid or a chamber of coffins. With nothing more than his intuition, he wandered this way and that. He had the idea to mark where he'd been, but beyond struggling what to mark his way with, he was scared that something would find his trail and follow it to find him instead. The list of things to fear had only been growing since he entered the cave, and he wanted to avoid any more confrontations at all costs.

This went on for some time, more than he could keep track of. Ever since he escaped his coffin, his sense of time was inconsistent at best. What felt like hours could've very well been days. Without the sun or a clock, there was no way to confirm. More than once, he saw the lights down one of the halls shift to bright pink, and he could hear the familiar sounds of a giggling woman and a shambling beast behind her. Each time he kept his distance. The only thing that could make this worse would be to get caught again. He tried to keep some semblance of strategy to his decisions, but his mind was faltering. He was tired, he was shivering uncontrollably, every crackle of the torches made him jump in fear, and the ever-present thirst continued to grind at his sanity. He needed to recover, but the brief rests he allowed himself consisted of him ducking into a dark room, huddling in the corner, and trying to keep his teeth from chattering too loudly. There was no chance of good sleep in this place—not outside of a coffin. He stared at them as he sat with a sense of both dread and envy. The sleep was not peaceful, but at least it was sleep. In there, he didn't have to worry about being attacked by whatever it was that kept patrolling the halls.

After a while, he continued again. Maybe he was doomed to never escape. Perhaps this is where it all ended for him. Wouldn't that be what he deserved? All this to save Ashley. He would do it again in a heartbeat, but what if he couldn't succeed in the end? What if he failed now like he failed in life? As her husband, it was his job to protect her, to make sure nothing bad happened to her. She was the most important thing in his life, and he let her down. If she'd have just kept an open mind and not been so closed off to new ideas, then none of this would've happened. So many moments she refused to just listen to reason, and he didn't press her. Was he too soft?

Everyone who knew her loved her, but she did rub a lot of people the wrong way. In the end, Josep had put the blame for that on her parents. They were just as dogmatic as she was, if not more. At least, she was willing to have dinner with people she disagreed with. He thought back to one specific dinner with a couple Josep had met at work. Ashley's parents happened to be visiting but refused to stay when they heard who was coming. Josep was so embarrassed. Ashley even tried to convince them to stay, but they insisted on going out so they wouldn't have to see them together, like they were some kind of monsters or something, too disgusting to even look at. Josep had seen real monsters now and was all the more certain that those men were not monsters. He couldn't recall their names now that he tried to. That had been so many years ago now.

As he wandered aimlessly, lost in thought, he didn't realize the faint glow around the corner. He turned without checking and was enveloped in pink light. He snapped back to reality and could see the shadow of a woman very close to him now, her back toward him, hovering two feet off the ground. He could just make out the disgusting flesh of a creature on the other side of her. Silently, eyes aghast, he backpedaled as fast as he could manage without tripping over himself. The monster was too enveloped by the woman to notice the trembling figure of Josep ducking back to the hall he had come from, or so it seemed when there was no immediate reaction.

Ears pounding, Josep rushed as fast as he could, still leaning heavily against the wall for support. He was in the thick of the pink field now. There was no chance of him making it to the end of the hall before the pair would be in sight. With mere moments to react, he dove into the first room he could reach. He glanced back as he did and saw that the woman was already in sight. Luckily, it seemed her gaze was transfixed on the thing tailing her, her fingers beckoning it to follow. The room he had hurried into was one with a pool. He very nearly fell in headfirst but caught himself just as one foot splashed in the liquid. Immediately, a wave of warmth rippled up his leg and through his body. There was a mixture of shooting pain and wonderful relief from the cold he had suffered until now. It was a shock he would have found most pleasant had he not been so near death in that moment. There were few places to hide in the empty room. He feverishly inspected the room and saw that on either side of the entrance was a very dark corner. Without hesitation, he pressed himself into one. It was only about a foot or two across. He wasn't concealed fully, or really very much at all, but he was determined to make it work. With all his might, he squeezed himself tightly into the corner, feeling very much like a roach hiding from a boot. His heart was racing. His toes were less than an inch away from the edge of the pool that filled the room. Their sounds were growing louder. Indeed, it seemed they turned the corner he had and were coming this way.

The woman's gleeful chuckling was clearer now than he'd ever heard it. Unfortunately, so was the creature's moaning. The lights were brighter now than they'd ever been; the pink glow spilled into the room darkening the shadows all the more. The sounds grew louder and louder until finally a wave of darkness drifted by the door. To Josep's horror, the woman floated into the room. He was certain his heart stopped beating then and there. He could see her shifting figure perfectly now as she was floating only a few feet away from him. She truly was like an inky black shadow. She was somewhat translucent, and her outline was hard to distinguish clearly. What he could make out clearly was her beauty. Her hair was floating as if she was underwater; tendrils grasped at the air all around her. She had her eyes locked at the doorway—at what Josep truly feared in this moment. She hovered back until she was over the center of the pool, still beckoning the creature to follow.

As it entered the room, its stench filled the air. Josep instinctively covered his mouth to stop himself from gagging. It was a pungent smell that was somehow familiar but far stronger than anything a human could produce. Its oily skin was loose in odd places, nearly sagging to the floor the lower Josep looked as if the poor man had started melting and stopped halfway. The realization hit Josep like a train; this was a man, or had been at some point. No one would've been able to realize had they not been so terrifyingly close.

From this distance, though, Josep recognized very clearly that this had once been a human, just as Josep was now. His arms outstretched toward the shadow of the woman, Josep could now hear words hidden deep in the moaning, "More…please…more!" Mindlessly, over and over, the man repeated his plea. Somehow neither the man nor the woman noticed Josep; either that or they simply ignored him. The woman called, and the man answered. As her gesture continued, she began to sink into the pool, and the man shuffled in after her, dragging a large hunk of the flesh between his legs on the ground behind him.

The pool started very shallow, but quickly, the man sunk lower and lower until both he and the shadow had disappeared into the viscous fluid. Paralyzed, Josep stared until the pool had calmed. As it did, the lights outside returned to their familiar green hue, and Josep's body was his again. Sticking to the wall, he slid into the hall and collapsed onto the floor. In those moments, he had forgotten completely about the cold, the thirst, everything. He felt lightheaded now, realizing he likely hadn't taken a breath since he hid. He allowed himself that luxury and sat there gasping. He wiped away the cold sweat that was teetering at the edge of his brow. He had to get out of here. For Ashley and himself. What could have caused a man to become something so grotesque? Could he even be considered alive in that state—as a mindless abomination? The sheer confusion swirled within the terror he had been growing accustomed to and stirred a new kind of determination within him. He wouldn't let whatever happened to these people happen to him. Ashley was waiting. Now paying much closer attention to the lights around him and peeking around every corner with a new sense of caution, Josep pressed on.

Something changed. Josep had been wandering without a goal for a very long time. Time meant strangely little to him at this point in his journey. He was haggard, beyond exhausted, and had nearly forgotten what it was like to have feeling in his extremities. Despite the lack of any visual changes, the slight feeling of warmth set off alarms in his mind immediately. It was only a very small thing, a brief pocket of heat that swept over his foot. But he felt it. His will had not wavered in this time. He was still dead set on his goal. However, in spite of his best efforts, his mind struggled to cope. The sudden tingle sent waves throughout his body, and he nearly shouted at the surprise. He was still wandering hallways that all looked the same, but this was new. Without sleep, he felt his sanity slipping away, but his body didn't work the same as it used to. Without food, rest, or water, he had continued to recover. Without any hesitation, his body running on instinct, he broke into a sprint or something like it.

After a few dozen yards, he felt another twinge of warmth graze his skin. He was escaping. With each corner he turned, he could feel, more and more. As if life itself was being pumped into his veins, the temperature began to approach something a man could cope with. He could no longer see his gasps as little clouds, and their absence was pure joy. Suddenly, he turned one last corner, and it was truly warm. Warm enough for his body at least. Without warning, his consciousness retreated. He had been past his limit for far longer than any living being could stand. Now that he could, his body demanded rest. He turned into the first room he came to and collapsed in the corner by a row of coffins. In an instant, he was gone.

Josep awoke. It only took a moment to realize where he was and remember his situation. He sat up slowly. His face had been firmly planted against the floor and a veritable river of drool had formed. He was still groggy but nowhere near what he had been prior to his sleep. He patted his face forcing himself to fully wake. It appeared nothing had discovered him while he slept. Somehow, he was still okay. His body ached, and he had to move slowly at first to work out the kink in his neck, but he was alive. When he finally tried standing, he was surprised; he had a sizable bruise that had formed on his hip due to how he collapsed on the floor, but he felt nearly fully restored. He was nothing like comfortable; in fact, he was miserable, but his body didn't seem to notice. If anything, he was just as capable now as he had been when his journey began. This was a peculiar thing to him. It would have drawn more attention earlier if he had the time or energy to pay it any. Now that he took the time to analyze his condition, he was astounded. He knew he should've been dead—but then again, he was. He had never considered what his body would be like after death. He'd just as well assumed that he'd have the same body he died with. This one was very similar in appearance to the one he'd had in his younger days but completely different in its performance.

Unfortunately, the one thing that never relented was the thirst. It was a state of being now. He had very nearly forgotten the taste of water at all. His lips were cracked, and breathing through his mouth was a certain way to cause him more pain. Most of the suffering he had been able to manage in some small way. The thirst was the one thing he could not overcome, though. He wondered why that, of all things, would be what caused him the most agony. Regardless, there was nothing he wouldn't give for water; that he knew for sure.

Finally back to his feet, stretched and fully awake, he prepared to continue. He was overjoyed by any change but had no idea how close to an exit he might be. Again, cautious as ever, though with far more dexterity, he peeked around the corner of the doorway. Confirming he was still alone, he ventured out. It only took another half hour or so of walking, still following the gradually increasing temperature, before he truly did find something new. He turned a corner and faced a very different hallway. It was half the length of what he had been used to for so long now. There was a dark room at the end and no passages to either side. It was almost too much of a shock. The hall looked bizarre to him now. Anything new was a strange and distant memory.

He stood there processing for far longer than the hall deserved. To him, this was a paradise. Good or bad, he was desperately grateful for any variation from the monstrous monotony he had been in. He cautiously continued to the doorway and peered inside. It took some time for his eyes to adjust. The only light he could see was from the green torches at his back. The room he was looking into now was very large indeed. He couldn't make out any walls or the ceiling. Anything was better than what he had been in; it had to be, so he dared to enter.

For the first few feet, he was walking blind. There were shapes all about, but he couldn't make them out clearly. He didn't detect any movement, and there wasn't a sound to be heard. He inched toward one of the shapes at the edge of his vision. Squinting in the dark, his eyes slowly adjusting to the dim, ethereal light, the shape slowly cleared. It was a square pedestal sitting roughly half his height with some sort of statue standing on top. The shape was vaguely human but abstract and nonspecific. He inspected it more closely but only confirmed it was made of stone. He slowly ventured deeper into the room and realized how many of these pedestals there were. Rows upon rows of pedestals all with their own statues. His eyes were now adjusted as they were going to be, but he could only see clearly a few yards in any direction. Only hazy shadows lurked further in the distance. He tried to keep his breathing quiet so as not to disturb the silence around him. The air was stagnant. There was a light coming from somewhere but he couldn't find the source. He idly inspected each statue as he passed. They were all completely unique, but all were simple shapes merely alluding to the human form. Some simply sat crisscross; some posed as if in the middle of a dance. His head swiveled back and forth, still cautious of any sign of danger.

More than once, he thought one of the statues seemed to move for a moment but confirmed it was his mind playing tricks. Then something did catch his eye; further ahead was the shape of a woman, a real woman standing on one of the pedestals. She wasn't moving, but she was the only clear shape in a sea of abstraction. She had to be real. Josep wasn't close enough to know for sure. He ducked behind one of the pedestals nearest him, keeping an eye locked on her form. He sat there for a moment, waiting, but so did she.

Were his eyes really playing tricks on him? Staying low to the ground, he waddled closer to her, back and forth between hiding places. Less than ten feet away, he could finally see that she was indeed a statue, made of the same stone as the rest. He breathed a sigh of relief. Then one of frustration. He'd just left a labyrinth of monotony that he'd grown accustomed to. He wasn't looking to find himself in a new one. She did look real though. Her shapes were smooth and exquisitely detailed. Close enough to touch her now, he could even make out pores along her skin. He reached out and laid a hand on her leg. There was no reaction, only cold stone. Josep walked around to see her face only to find it blank. As if someone had created this wondrously life-like sculpture only to leave the final touch as a blank, unfashioned rock. The question occurred to Josep as to what these were, and why they were here. The woman stared into the void, frozen in time. Josep glanced around. He'd been moving in a straight line without any goal in sight. He could still see the way he'd come in, now only a tiny, green square in the distance. What was the point of all of this? He turned back the way he was heading and continued.

After only a few feet, he noticed another shape that was much clearer than the rest as well. Approaching slowly, it was another woman, this one poised like a ballerina. Her face was blank as well, betraying the wondrous detail everywhere else. While wondering how her weight was balanced without any supports, he heard a noise in the distance. He turned toward it, eyes wide. It was only a momentary crack that had come and gone. It was stone on stone whatever it was, but there was no movement he could see anywhere. It sounded like it was far off from where he now crouched, but regardless, it wasn't something he wanted to learn more about.

Fortunately, it wasn't the direction he had been moving, so he continued, now lower to the ground. It honestly couldn't be helping much, trying to hide behind the pedestals; it was far too dark for anything to reasonably notice him as long as he didn't make any noise. Regardless, he moved low and as fast as he could manage without making a sound. He didn't take the time to admire the statues anymore. Quick glances were all he afforded them while he kept his attention on the direction the noise had come from. It seemed like more of the statues were complete now, though. Nearly every statue he took notice of was a similarly intricate sculpture of a faceless woman. He passed by a dozen, a new one every few yards, as he crept through the shadows. One was posed as a woman in prayer, the next as a stage performer, the next reclining on the ground. They faced this way and that without any sense of order or purpose. Ashley was kneeling with her face in her hands.

Josep froze in a panic and looked back at what he'd just hurried past. The form he'd nearly ignored was a sculpture of Ashley, or so it seemed. Her face was covered and so it looked to be almost like the real thing sitting there atop the pedestal. "Ashley," Josep whispered to himself inaudibly. He moved toward her statue. It had to be her. His mind had faltered numerous times in his wanderings thus far. He realized some time ago that he'd all but forgotten what most of his friends' names were. But he knew every curve, every hair, every inch of Ashley. This had to be her. Even in stone, it was uncanny.

It took him more than a few moments to convince himself it wasn't truly her sitting atop the stone block. He reached out and felt her form, hoping against hope that it would be her. He caressed the cold stone, his eyes welling up. He had never forgotten her, but somehow, she was more beautiful than ever before. He had to find her, the real her. This trick of the light was torment, and he wouldn't forgive it. Eyes locked on her form, he desperately wished he could see her face.

A voice whispered from behind, "Josep."

He spun around. The voice was feminine and otherworldly, almost musical. He saw nothing yet again, only the shapes of women lined up as far as he could make out. Another whisper from his right, "Josep." Like a siren calling to a ship, the voice was beautiful and sultry but betrayed a malevolent intent.

Without pause, he crawled away from the voice, shuffling as low as he could without sacrificing speed. His heart was beginning to race now. He wouldn't be caught again. Far off ahead of him, the voice echoing off the walls he couldn't see, "Josep." It was a whisper that traveled like a wave throughout the cavern.

"Where are you, Josep?"

He did his best to keep a pedestal between him and the voice or voices. It seemed to come from a new place every time it called everywhere except where he was shuffling to. Each time it called, the voice rung in his ears, "Josep…come back, Josep."

He kept moving, shutting the sounds out. His heart was pounding, and his efforts at keeping calm were wavering. He had no idea where his pursuers were or what they were. He remembered the shadows of the women who led the beasts into their warm pools.

He wouldn't let himself be caught again. He wouldn't go back to that suffering. His breathing was rapid now. "Josep...Josep...Josep." Every few seconds, a new voice whispered in the dark, beckoning him back.

No...no. I'm not going back. The thought repeated in his mind like a mantra, *Ashley. I have to save Ashley.*

Then her voice called, "Josep."

For an instant, he paused. His heart stopped, and everything was right in the world. She'd called his name. He hadn't heard her voice in so long. He needed to hear it. But it wasn't her. It couldn't be.

"Josep, where are you?"

He wanted to call out to her, the real her. He wouldn't fail. He wouldn't get caught. He rushed on. The figures of women flashed by in his periphery.

"I'm not going back. I have to find her."

Her voice called again and again, "Josep...Josep."

"It's not her. Get out. I have to get out." He covered his ears, but the cries wouldn't cease. He was in a cold sweat now. He was running, doubled over trying to feign secrecy.

"Josep, you wouldn't leave me again, Josep, would you?" Her voice was everywhere. She was everywhere. He couldn't escape. His ears were ringing. His head was pounding.

"Leave me alone. I'm not going back. I have to save her." He screamed the thoughts in his mind, but it wouldn't drown out the summons.

"Come back, Josep. Don't leave me again. Josep...Josep...Josep!"

It had to stop. It had to. His thoughts grew too loud in defiance until he screamed out loud, "SHUT UP!"

Instantly, light filled the void. A familiar, pale blue static blinded him in a flash. His head turned, and he froze in place. A huge blue screen blared in the distance casting a spotlight on him. The silhouettes of the statues stretched hundreds of yards in the distance, their shadows now stretched long and black all over the room. Her voice became a guttural screech from the screen, "JOSEP!" He bolted onward. In the light, he could now see a doorway ahead only a few hundred feet away. The light came to life, shaking all over.

The sounds of the beast crashing through statues reverberated all throughout the chamber. He glanced toward it only for a moment as he sprinted. He saw shadows of her massive clawed hands scrambling through the field of sculptures, broken pieces flying all around. Her voice was now an animal shriek that hung in the air.

Josep's roar was drowned out by the sound, "I'm not going back!"

The shattering grew closer and closer, but he was already through. He dashed through the door and into the darkness. It was far too small of an exit for the monster to pass through, but that gave him no pause. Before the light vanished behind him, he saw the shapes of unrefined tunnels and knew he was near the exit now. He had no guesses as to what direction, and he was now in complete darkness. He continued his sprint, fueled by adrenaline and terror. The tunnels were smaller now but not small enough to keep the creature out. He remembered how she squeezed and slithered through corridors long ago when he was first captured. "I'm getting out. I'm getting out," he kept muttering to himself over and over, running in the blackness.

He felt himself begin to collide with the side of the wall and corrected, now keeping his hand outstretched to trace along the tunnel's edge. Without breaking pace, he continued as fast as he could. The static and the light had disappeared behind him but only for a minute or so. There was no light, but somewhere far behind him, he heard the noise approaching again. She would find him if he relented. He wouldn't let himself. He wasn't injured, but he hadn't pushed himself to run this hard in ages, and it showed.

After only a very short time, he was heaving, his lungs burning for air. His pace slowed, but only a little. The tunnel curved to the left before it quickly ended, and he ran headlong into a wall. He landed on his back hard. He didn't feel anything break but was far too panicked to really tell. Still heaving, he forced himself up, reached out blindly until he felt the wall ahead of him, and then turned to his right and continued. His run was more of a limp for a few moments, but he was determined to push through the pain. He sped up again, now keeping one arm against the wall on his left and the other stretched out in front of him. Still without light, he had no clue what was coming next, but it had to be better than where he had been. The static grew quieter for a moment, but before he allowed himself to slow, it grew louder yet again. His hunter knew these tunnels and was scouring them far faster than he was. He was a rat in a maze and felt as such. His head was screaming now from the impact and the exertion. Had it been hours or only seconds? His focus was solely on the sound of the static behind him and now on the scraping sounds of her claws against the stone.

Her pounding echoed through the tunnels, and for a moment, he thought he saw flashes of blue light coming from behind. He had to get out. He couldn't get caught again. The path twisted and turned this way and that. Slow curves one way followed by sharp turns the other. He turned down hallways at random, skipping some and taking others. There was no plan or strategy; he simply had to escape. Then, by some miracle, he turned a corner and saw a dim green light ahead. Had he really come all this way to find his way back to where he began? It didn't matter. Anywhere was better than here.

His sprint truly was a desperate limp now. He threw his body forward with each lumbering stride. He'd closed half the distance when a new light came into view. The ghostly blue spotlight had found him. The static was very loud now. He could hear her clawing at the floor and walls, pulling herself through the tight passageway. His chest was on fire, but he wouldn't relent. He forced new energy into his steps. The light was very close now. His long black shadow was changing shape as she grew closer too. He reached the light and turned hard to his left following the path he'd come in through only to see a wall. There were passageways all around him, but the way he'd entered was no longer there.

In an instant, his heart sank, and every fiber of his being screamed in silent panic. He spun around to find the light of the exit behind him. She was very close now. The tunnel grew smaller and smaller, yet she pursued. He gave everything he had in the last stretch of his race. It was so very close now. The orange glow from outside was bright as daylight compared to where he'd been. He felt a long nail scrape along his back and nearly hook his shirt as she raked the ground. She reached one last time as he dove through the exit, her hand the only thing small enough to fit through the doorway. He landed on the gravel hard and tumbled down a very slight hill before coming to a stop.

He was completely exhausted, his sweat nearly blinding him. He looked back with blurred vision to see the monster's hand blocking the way he'd come, clawing this way and that, trying to feel for him. He was outside her reach now, though. He had escaped. He lay there on his back gasping for air with the black void above him, the screams of suffering around him in the distance, and the flickering orange glow illuminating the space around him. The sulfurous gas he was breathing burned his lungs all the more, but in this moment, it was a welcome pain.

After a few more moments of fruitless clawing, the hand slithered back into its cave and was gone for good. He was outside. Josep didn't even give a thought to where he had landed or what was around him. His relief was boundless, and he relished the moment. He lay on the ground with his eyes closed until his breathing slowly returned to normal. Whatever came next had to be better than where he had been.

TEN

After a few precious minutes of rest, Josep opened his eyes. He was sweating profusely now that he had returned to the heat of the outside. Although strangely, the sweltering was something of a comfort now after what seemed like an eternity in the frigid labyrinth. His breathing had normalized, save the involuntary coughing as his body attempted to reject the toxic vapors around him. He had been laying on sharp gravel, and what began as a relatively comfortable landing was growing more painful with each moment. In spite of it all, though, he was outside, and he was grateful. He stood to his feet and had to tread carefully on his new footing. This was someplace he had not been. His suspicion that he had exited the way he entered was incorrect. Josep stood on a similar branch of the giant, gnarled tree of dark stone that he had before the cave; however, this one was on the other side as far as he could tell. He was much further down now, and the massive stone column he had escaped from towered far above him into the darkness. The flames at the base of the tree were much hotter now than they had been before.

He peered over the edge but only could stand it for a moment. The orange glare shone brightly as flickers of shadows tumbled off the tree and into the flames. He was still very, very far above the fire itself. Without checking, he would have never been able to tell, though. The underside of the colossal tree's branches had a glint of red as the heat baked the stone. Turning away from the cave, the path continued a short ways until it came to another spiraling stairwell, very narrow and very tall. He gingerly stepped across the bridge, trying to spare his bare feet as much pain as he could, given the unwelcoming ground.

The tower the staircase sat inside was poorly constructed, to put it generously. It was made of the same dark, glimmering stone the coliseum had been. Random segments and chunks of the walls were missing and gave way to a very long fall. Without any sort of consistent railing, Josep resorted to sitting on each step as he slowly made his way down. On more than one occasion, he nearly slid down more than one step at a time and had to catch himself. Sections of the stairs themselves were crumbled away and weren't easy to see in advance. Eventually, he did reach the bottom unharmed. When he did, he found a very new sight. Attached to the stairwell's exit was another short gravel bridge that led to a rickety, iron gate. One door hung open, looking like it would fall off its hinges at any moment. Beyond the thin bars sat a very dismal, gray town. The dirt street stretched far into the distance ahead and far off to Josep's left. Most of the buildings were two stories tall at most, aside from a few strange towers in the distance that stretched all the way up to the nightmarish clouds that hung overhead. They looked more like smog than honest clouds, but they hovered over the entirety of the town and far off into the horizon.

The orange glow from below made them swirl with wicked hues filling Josep with a sense of dread. He walked to the gate and slipped through the opening. The gate made a loud squeak even at his slight disturbance. He stood now on the dirt road, happy to be off the gravel. The buildings were more like burnt-out shacks up close. The black timbers had crumbled long before Josep had ever come to this place. Some buildings were entirely collapsed, and piles of cinders sat all about. There was still no wind in the slightest, and it was only now that Josep noticed the silence. He could still hear the roar of the flames below, but it seemed somehow muffled once he'd passed the gate. The choir of pain that filled the atmosphere wherever he went was now all but gone entirely. It was strangely still and painfully quiet. He noticed a particular flash in the veil above and caught a glance at a flash of red lightning that arced between the clouds. It was only a small thing, but it made an even smaller noise. The slightest rumble met his ears. He saw no signs of life and dared to make a sound himself, "Hello?" He intended to speak in a hushed tone but spoke far softer than intended; it seemed almost sacrilege to break the silence in this place. Louder this time, "Anyone there?"

His voice traveled through the streets and was met very quickly with a panicked response, "Shh!" The hush came from one of the piles of ash just to his right. He turned quickly, alert at first, until he saw the man who had responded. He was dressed—using the term *loosely*—in burnt rags and sat curled up in a pile beside one of the ruined structures. Josep would have never realized he was alive had the man not made himself known; he blended in with the landscape of gloom all too well as if he belonged to it. This was the first real human Josep had seen since entering this place. It had been so long since he'd had the chance to speak with anyone; he didn't know where to begin. Regardless, the man did not seem interested in conversation in the least. He seemed almost dismissive like he was annoyed with Josep's presence more than anything. The man only gave him a glance before his gaze returned to the dust he sat in. Josep hesitated but couldn't resist an attempt. In a hushed tone, "I'm sorry. I'm looking for—"

He'd barely begun his question before the man hushed him again, more forcefully this time. Josep had few options, though, and was determined to get something resembling directions from what could very well be his only source of information for a very long time. He tried again, quieter still. "Look, I need your help." He took a few steps closer to make sure the man could hear his plea.

The man quickly shot back again, "Shut up! Just shut up! I don't care. You have to shut up, or you're going to get us both in trouble, and I'm not getting punished for you." The man's voice was strained. He seemed strong enough physically, but it sounded as if he hadn't spoken in quite some time. He choked on his words, determined to make sure his point was made. Another muffled rumble followed a dim flash of red light in the distance.

Josep continued, "I'm not going to get you in trouble. But I need your help! I don't know where I'm going. I need to find my—" A different sort of rumble shook the ground.

Before Josep could turn to face it, the man rushed out a hurried response, "The other side all right! Go to the other side. Just go away! Leave me alone!" Eyes widened in fear, he scrambled backward through the ash and disappeared behind one of the ruins. Josep turned around as another rumble echoed out. It took a moment to process what was happening. One of the black spires that stretched into the clouds above was moving. What Josep had seen as a tower was, in fact, a very tall, slender creature with needle-like arms and legs. Each step closer it took sent shockwaves through the city. There was no head Josep could see, only patches of discoloration in odd shapes across its torso. It was a colossal thing, where only moments ago, it had been roughly a mile away; it was nearly on him now.

It took long deliberate strides that made it seem as if it was moving in slow motion. It was bending below the canopy of smog and heading directly where Josep now stood. In a panic, Josep ran to follow the man who had shuffled away into one of the burnt-out buildings. He turned the corner and ducked quickly to crawl through a hole into what was left of a room. Dim shafts of red light crept in through the holes in the structure. Another two rumbles shook the world, and bits of the ceiling crumbled with each one. The shadow of the thing covered the structure as it loomed above. Josep chose the darkest corner he could find and huddled into it tightly. There was a pause of silence before the giant began to make a very loud and bizarre noise. The sound shook the structure so much Josep felt it might cave in entirely. The noise was so alien in nature Josep couldn't place it in the slightest. To him, it sounded mechanical at first but guttural and with a sort of subtle sucking that was sickening to hear.

As it continued, it became sort of rhythmic to an extent, following a loop that lasted far longer than Josep would've liked. The noise eventually subsided, and all was quiet again. The shadow still covered the building, and Josep sat there frozen, committed to his hiding place until the thing went away. Then, a very quiet whimper broke the silence. Josep could just make out the shadow of the other man move from a dark place on the far side of the room. He slipped through an opening in the far wall and disappeared. From his silhouette, Josep could just tell that the man was covering his mouth. Josep did the same without knowing why. A few moments went by again in a very heavy, tense silence before a scream tore it to shreds.

Josep could only imagine it was the same man, but he had no way of knowing. In either case, the shadow of the creature shifted as it stood up and moved away toward the scream, its footsteps thundering as it went. Another quick scream echoed out before abruptly ending. The giant's footsteps stopped, the screaming was gone, and the world fell silent again. Josep sat in the thick quiet for quite some time after. He was alone again, with only his thoughts and the odd roll of thunder that rang out every few minutes. Staying here was no good, but leaving didn't sound any better. When his heart had slowed again, he reminded himself he had no choice and told himself the lie that once he found Ashley, then everything would be okay. He knew even then he'd have to find a way out, and as time went on, that hope seemed more like a fantasy. If he was doomed to stay in this place forever, though, he would do it with her. This would not stop him.

Josep eventually built up the courage to check outside his ramshackle hiding place. Fortunately, the dirt and ash made for a quiet floor to cross. He went to the opening the stranger had left through and slowly peeked around the corner. There were less than ten feet of space between the room he was hiding in and the next ruined structure. In that gap, though, was one of the giant's spindly legs. Josep's gaze followed it up and saw the creature had frozen in place in a bent-over position. One of its arms looked to be resting on the ground, but it was out of view behind the next building. The leg closest to

Josep truly grew to a fine point; there was no foot but rather a razor-like tip that sank deep into the ground. Its nearby *footsteps* were simple holes nearly five feet deep but only a foot or so across at a glance. The thing had its back to Josep, and regardless, there weren't any eyes that he could make out in the first place. How the thing found him in the first place was something Josep could only guess at.

Josep nearly turned around to move around the creature the long way but had an urge to see what had happened to his short-lived companion. The screams had been him, surely, but if he could somehow save him, he might have a much-desired ally for the rest of the journey. The thought had crossed his mind that the man was dead. Could someone truly die in this place, though? Was that even a possibility?

After so much time here, Josep possessed a pitiful amount of information. Even if it was only a slim chance, he had to at least confirm the man's condition. Against his better judgment, Josep slowly crept across the gap between structures, giving the monstrous leg as wide a birth as he could manage. He jumped to finish the last few feet, despite the creature making no movements whatsoever. Josep had no idea if the thing could see at all, but he had no desire to find out.

The next building was very much like the first; the interior walls had all but disappeared, leaving a single large room. The walls were riddled with holes and left an uncomfortably small amount of cover. The monster's figure could be seen through the gaps. Sticking to the patches of shadow that split the room, Josep made his way toward the other side to see where the giant's hand met the ground. He didn't get a good look until he was nearly touching the wall; when he did, the small hope he had at gaining a companion was lost.

The stranger was lying face down in the dirt. The giant's arm ended the same way his legs did in a single fine point, only this arm had impaled the man and pinned him to the ground. Josep couldn't see his face but saw his arm reaching out for help that didn't exist. His fingers twitched every few seconds like an insect fighting for life long after its end had come. A pang of guilt filled Josep's chest. He hadn't meant to, of course. He only wanted help. The excitement of finding another living soul had overcome his reason. And yet, the consequences of his ignoring the man's warning lay in front of him. The pool of blood slowly continued to grow around the man's body. It wasn't Josep's fault. Of course, he didn't mean to; if he'd only known the danger.

It took a moment to even realize what was happening next. Without a sound, figures began to emerge from other alleys and streets. Animal skulls sat atop tall, thin humanoid figures. The giant's hulking form dwarfed everything around it, but these things still stood at an intimidating eight feet or so. They didn't walk so much as float toward the body. Bits of tattered cloth, or flesh, hung from their forms as they drifted silently toward their prey. Josep counted seven before the first reached the man's still-twitching body. The beast came to rest over the man's form ever so softy before calmly and deliberately ripping bits of his body apart and feasting on his remains. The man's limbs came off with gut-wrenching pops and snaps. The creatures put in very little effort to separate the chunks they wanted.

Josep could only stomach to watch a few seconds before he turned away in horror and disgust. His heart was beating madly now, and his body broke out into a feverish sweat. How many of these creatures were there in this place? Even as they feasted, they made a disturbingly small amount of noise. The only sound that reminded Josep of what was happening behind this wall was the cracking and popping of bone and sinew. He felt his stomach begin to turn, and he thought he would hurl if not for the petrifying feeling that he would be caught if he did.

He had to get away from the sound though and these things. With his limbs trembling uncontrollably and his heart beating like a drum in his ears, he crawled on all fours back the way he came. He exited this ruin and reentered the one he had come from. With enough distance between him and the horror happening behind him, he settled into a corner to calm himself. It took a concerted effort to keep himself from throwing up, but he managed. He stared wide-eyed at the floor. The image of the macabre feast was burned into his mind. This was very bad. He had no other option than to brave this town of nightmares. He refused to consider returning to the cave. He would welcome death rather than return to that place. But a death like this? He tried his best to put the thought from his mind. He still had his goal, his quest. Ashley was in here somewhere. The image of Ashley's body replacing the strangers flashed in his mind for an instant, and he nearly screamed. No, he wouldn't allow that. He held fast to his resolve.

He anchored himself to the one thing that had kept him sane throughout all of this so far. He would find her, and they would make it out. Of that, there could be no doubt. He had suffered too much already. How much more had she been through already? He couldn't imagine it, and he didn't want to. He would prevail; they would prevail. After all, he had right on his side.

That didn't help him here and now, though. He considered simply sprinting through the town to try and find the exit and put this place behind him as soon as possible. The beasts seemed slow enough; it was the giants that concerned him. When he'd first entered this place, he noted the dozens of black spires that pierced the skyline. This giant had been one of those spires, so it only made sense that they all would come to life if provoked. The stranger's pleas for silence told Josep now that he needed to simply be quiet, and he would be all right. That's what he told himself now, anyway. He wasn't sure he believed it, but he had to.

Without any other choice but to continue, there was nothing else he could do. He finally pulled himself to his feet and crept to the wall closest to the street. He peeked out through the gaps to survey his surroundings. He could see the side of the giant's form still hunched over the same place it had been. The place the beasts had congregated was just out of view behind the building Josep had left. There had been no sounds, but the things moved so quietly that it wasn't much help in telling where they might be. As long as he was quiet, he should be fine. He repeated that sentiment to himself in his head over and over. The stranger told him the exit was on "the other side." Josep's only guess as to where that might refer to was the other side of the town from where he'd entered.

The street stretched far into the distance to his right where the feast was going on. Josep moved through the ruin until he was nearly back to the gate he had come in through. Now he could see the other direction available to him. The same dirt road ran by the gate and continued far off into the distance. The gate sat in the corner of what he could only guess was a large square city. Aside from the massive giants that stood scattered throughout the buildings, there were no landmarks of note. He was terrified to begin for fear that the beasts would see him crossing the road. It took an amount of time he wasn't proud of, but eventually, he built up the courage to attempt it. He gingerly leaned out of his hiding place until he could see where the giant had pinned the stranger. It had been some time since he had looked at the site but hoped the creatures would still be occupied with their meal.

When he leaned out enough to get a good look, he saw the group had grown. It was a pile of bodies from this distance and hard to make out individual forms, but where there had been seven or so before, there were nearly triple that number now. They were pressed up against one another in a horrifically calm feeding frenzy. There could only be scraps at this point, but Josep wouldn't let the opportunity to pass by unseen go to waste. He had slowly been covered in ash and soot simply by sitting in the ruins but was desperate to go unseen.

Josep found a sizable pile of ash nearby and covered himself until he was one consistent shade of gray camouflage. He peeked out again to confirm the creatures were distracted before he lay flat on the ground and started dragging himself through the dirt toward the other side of the street. He was far enough away, and their backs were toward him, but he refused to be caught in the open. He crawled as fast as he could manage without making too much noise. When he made it to the other side, he wasted no time scrambling to his feet and ducking into another burned-out structure. He made his way through the room, through piles of dust and ash, and around the remains of fallen-down walls and ceiling until he could squeeze through a gap in the opposing wall and into the adjacent building. This went on for some time as Josep made his way through the silent city. He moved with purpose but gave priority to staying as quiet as possible.

The rumble of thunder high above him was the only sound he heard or wanted to hear. The noises around him still seemed somehow muffled, but even so, the creaks of a floorboard or the slight rustling of the dirt beneath his feet were enough to give him alarm. Fortunately, there were no sightings of the silent creatures as he went. There was no sign of life at all, in fact, for a number of miles.

He continued his routine of entering a building, scanning the shadows for any movement, slowly making his way to the other side, and finding a sizable gap to fit through. Josep entered the next building and had to muffle an instinctual scream. Before he had moved his head all the way through the gap he was entering, he saw a figure sitting in one of the shadowy corners of the next room. He took a moment to think before peeking in again. It wasn't a creature but was another person sitting huddled in the corner very much like the stranger he had met earlier.

Whoever this was, they didn't seem to notice him yet. It looked to be a woman, asleep and curled up tightly in one of the darker shadows in the room. It was then that Josep realized this was the first real woman he had seen since his journey began. Her dark hair was matted and tangled. She had some sort of torn fabric covering everything up to her neck. He watched as her breathing slowly raised and lowered her makeshift blanket. A thought occurred to him as he watched, something that seemed so obvious now, but he hadn't taken the time to realize. People—real human people—live in this place. He had seen monsters and horrors all throughout his journey thus far. He'd seen what had become of the men tormented and twisted in the cave. This woman and the stranger from earlier, however, were of a different sort. They hadn't thrown themselves into the fires below; they hadn't been caught and killed by the bloodthirsty beasts in the streets. How long had she been here in her squalor? Josep had been wandering for far longer than he could even guess at now, but he hadn't stopped or settled down anywhere for long. As far as Josep could tell, this is how she lived. When had she died? What was her life like? Was there someone in her life that meant as much as Ashley meant to him? Josep was different from the rest; he had been given the choice to come here. Did she have that choice, or was she simply put here against her will? A deep swelling of sympathy welled up inside him. She didn't deserve this, did she? What could someone possibly have done in life to deserve this without end? As far as Josep knew, she could have been a murderer or career criminal in life. She seemed so innocent now, though, alone in such a grim place.

He slowly pulled himself through the gap in the wall. As he did, his pants brushed against the charred wood of the structure. It didn't make much noise at all, and only a few bits of ash fell to the ground, but it was enough to rouse the woman. Her eyes shot open, and she scanned the room in an instant. Josep expected her to jump to her feet and flee like a frightened animal, but instead, she sat unmoving, eyes locked on the intruder to her hiding place. Neither made a sound. After a few moments, however, her eyes filled with tears, and she began to silently weep.

Josep began to motion as best he could that he had no intention of causing her any trouble. In spite of this, she continued, turning her gaze away. There was no hint of fear anymore, only a deep sorrow. Josep felt as if he'd done something wrong now; again, he seemed to be the cause of a stranger's grief no matter what he did. He felt another urge to help in some way, but what could he do? Perhaps the best thing he could do was to simply leave her alone and be on his way. He still had so many questions, but the fear of being discovered by the monsters that threatened every second of his time in this town kept him silent. He wouldn't risk his journey, nor this woman's safety on his account. He had to know why she was crying, though. Something in him was desperate to know. He hadn't done anything, and no threat had been made. It seemed as if the sight of him was enough to send her into a fit of despair. He wouldn't risk speaking to her, though.

Holding his hands up, trying his best to show his peaceful intent, he slowly moved just a bit closer. She didn't seem to mind this; she continued to weep, covering her mouth to muffle sounds, only giving him quick glances before pulling her eyes away again.

Once he'd come close enough, he squatted down next to a reasonably flat pile of ash and dust. With his finger, he began to write in the dirt.

WHY ARE YOU CRYING?

It occurred to him halfway through the message that she might not understand English. The people here were presumably from all different parts of the world and even all different times throughout history. Did she even understand writing at all? Hoping against hope, he finished the message anyways and looked to her for an answer. After a few more moments, when she could pull herself together well enough to look at the writing, she actually did begin to write a message back. She brushed away his writing and replaced it; her writing was shaky, and each letter was a wildly different size than the one before, but it was legible enough.

YOU

Josep didn't understand. What about him? He had guessed that he was the cause of her crying, but what was it about him? Was the sight of anyone enough to bring her to tears? He looked at her in confusion and found her staring at him. In that moment, eyes locked, Josep felt something he couldn't place. She reminded him of something or someone that he couldn't remember. Like trying to remember a dream from early childhood when one has grown into old age, he knew there was something to it but had no hope of placing what it was.

She could only hold her composure a few more seconds before her emotions overwhelmed her, and she returned to her weeping, trying her best to keep from making any real noise. Now curled more tightly than she had been before, she hid her face entirely. He didn't know what he had done, or who this woman had been, but he felt for her pain more than he thought he should. Without looking, she stretched out an arm and pointed to the far corner of the room. Looking over, Josep saw another gap in the far wall that continued in the direction he had been traveling. She was done talking. Again, he had more questions than answers. Even with another human right in front of him, he felt more alone now than he had during his entire odyssey. He didn't know this woman; he couldn't. He had never been here before and had never met her in life, not that he could remember anyways. Yet somehow, he knew this woman. He wanted more, but Ashley was waiting, and this woman seemed distressed by his very presence. As much as he resented the thought of never knowing the truth, he resigned to follow her instructions and leave her be.

Before he stood up, he put a hand on her shoulder. Whoever this woman was, his heart went out to her. After letting it rest a moment, he pulled himself to his feet and quietly shuffled his way to the exit she had directed him to. He glanced back once more to find her again staring at him, eyes full of tears and pity. He paused, hoping she would offer more. To his dismay, she again fell into hysterics and turned away. His heart heavier than ever, and without a reason why, he squeezed through the next gap and into the next narrow alleyway.

Josep stood there for a moment, lost in thought. He was sure he hadn't met the woman before, but that feeling kept nagging at his mind. It didn't take long before a dull ache began to form in his temples. His mind felt like a towel that had been wrung out far more than was worth it. The pain in his head began to highlight the other aches and pains he had, and soon, they all began to grow at once. He needed rest again. What little he had before was just enough to get him going, and by this point, he'd been wandering the silent city for what must have been a day or so. A part of him thought he should be used to the anxiety caused by ever-present danger after living with it for so long but somehow, it never seemed to go away, or even lessen.

Just as he thought this, a very loud crash sounded off toward the street on his left. In actuality, it might not have been very loud at all; but compared to the silence he had become accustomed to, it was an earth-shattering explosion. He almost ran away at that moment, but some morbid curiosity called to him. Attempting a compromise, his heart racing in panic, he dove into the ruins of the structure in front of him and, after confirming the room was empty, sidled his way to the front of the building to see if he could get a view of what had made the sound.

As he had before, he found a sizable series of gaps in the wall that had once formed the front of the building. Making sure to only step in the piles of ash and dirt that would dull his footsteps, he positioned himself to get the best view he could and almost immediately regretted it. Across the street and in front of the very house he'd found the woman in was a pack of the slender animal-headed beasts he had been dreading running into. They weren't facing her building but, rather, the building across from hers, which had apparently just collapsed. The entire group of a dozen or so stood in a semicircle, facing the newly formed pile of rubble. Each stood nearly eight feet tall and had sagging flaps of dark furry skin draped over their bodies. Whether it was some monstrous clothing or their actual flesh, Josep couldn't tell. One was positioned in the center of the formation and held a piece of burned lumber like a club. This creature had some sort of large feline skull atop its broad, bony shoulders and looked to have just finished a massive swing; its club was embedded in a shattered log that had once held the doorframe in place.

The entire group stood frozen in place and watched as the club-wielding creature removed its weapon, snapped it in half like a twig, and tossed it onto the pile of rubble. Before Josep had time to wonder what had led to the strange events taking place in front of him, things became much stranger. All at once, the semicircle turned about-face, and the one in the center lifted up its gnarled, six-fingered claw. A few moments passed until the creature slowly lowered one finger. Suddenly, there was rustling in the debris of the newly destroyed building. Two men and a woman hurriedly pulled themselves out of the ruins and scrambled to their feet. They were injured and bloodied but moved as fast as they could. The creature in the center slowly lowered another finger.

As the two men finished clambering out from under the broken planks, they immediately began to hurry away. The woman had nearly freed herself when she lurched to a stop. She began to pull at her leg which was still buried in the rubble. Her silence rapidly turned to panicked whimpering as she struggled to get loose. The creature lowered a third finger. The men had already left the woman on her own, their own terror outweighing any sense of pity they may have had. The woman didn't cry, though. She was terrified and panicked but resigned. Her effort to free herself waned within seconds, and her composure went with it.

What began as soft whimpering became full-fledged blubbering as she collapsed still half-buried under the ruin. Josep was panicked. It was too late now; even if he ran to her full sprint, there was no chance of freeing her and escaping unscathed. The creature lowered another finger, and with it, the entire procession crouched as if ready to pounce. He had to do something. If he cried out, maybe they would be distracted and leave her be. No, there were too many. Even if he drew all but one of them away, she would still be doomed. Maybe if he found some way to make a noise somewhere else. They would quickly find out he was the source, though, wouldn't they?

The woman was a miserable heap now, her head planted in her hands, violently weeping. Her muffled cries rang out through the streets. Josep noticed a few of the creatures' monstrous clawed toes anxiously tapping the ground as if they were downright giddy. The monster in the middle lowered yet another finger. Josep's head was swirling. How could those men leave her without a second's hesitation? She'd been in the building with them. Didn't they care enough to even try? They should've done something. He should do something. But what could he do? Too much time had passed before he'd even realized it. It was too late now. But he couldn't leave her, right? She needed help.

The creature began to lower its last evil finger, and as it did, a yelp sprung up from Josep's core and escaped his lips. His voice cracked as it was more of a squeak than a yell, but it was quite unintentional either way; or rather, he hadn't decided if he should make it or not. It was too late now, though. It was out, and it did not go unnoticed. The group of hunters had already begun to turn toward the woman when they heard Josep's cry. They all turned to face it in an instant. Josep turned and began to run as fast he could toward the back of the building before he could even see the creatures begin to give chase.

This was madness. What had he done? The trapped woman was surely just as doomed as she had been, and now he was in the same position. He aimed toward the biggest crack in the wall he could find, in the second he had, before he dove toward it. He crashed through the wall with ease and scrambled to his feet without missing a beat. The next wall was almost missing entirely, and then he was out on the street. He wasn't really concerned with where he was going. He hadn't even taken an instant to consider it, but without thinking, he was continuing down the way he had been traveling all this time. He sprinted down the dirt road between the ruined buildings as long as he could without daring a glance behind. A female scream echoed out behind, and he cringed when he heard it. He should've done more. He could've done more, but he'd been too afraid. His conscience tallied another victim he'd failed, and his eyes welled with tears. He knew this woman even less than the one in the building, but he felt a knife in his gut at the thought of leaving her to her fate. Just then he realized then that his cry without a source may have led the creatures to search the nearby buildings and find the woman he'd met there. This stopped him cold in his tracks. He screeched to a halt without even thinking and spun around quickly to see what was behind. To his dismay, he turned just in time to see two of the beasts leave the building he had left and turn to face him. They ran on all fours, but their movement seemed more like the shadows of a campfire flickering as they moved. Instinct took over again, and Josep returned to his sprint.

After another few seconds, he was already breathing heavily. His heart was pounding in his ears, and the sulfurous air choked his lungs. At the first indication that his speed was slowing, he found the first building with an opening he could, and he leaped inside. Without breaking stride, he ran to the opposite wall and slammed his shoulder into it. Most of it gave way, but a chunk stood relatively firm, and he stumbled as he broke through to the other side. Holding his arm tight now, he turned tight again and navigated his way through the ruined buildings, trying his best to make it difficult to follow him. Unfortunately, the creatures in pursuit made no noise as they gave chase, and so he had no way of knowing how far off they were—or how close.

Another few twists and turns and then very abruptly, the scenery changed. Josep ran out through the broken doorway in front of him and onto a street that simply ended. As if the entire city was cut in half, Josep now stood on the edge of the cliff with a simple iron gate sitting door ajar. For a brief moment, he stood still, absorbing the new site before he came to his senses. He was still in danger, and so he ran up to the gate. Only once he could touch it did he notice the very narrow staircase, carved into the side of the rock, that led down the cliff face. It was barely two feet across, however, and it was a long ways down.

The monstrous stone tree branch he had traveled all this time seemed to take a very sharp downward turn before resuming a more forgiving angle. Hundreds of feet below, Josep could see another narrow path that led to some new area he couldn't discern from here. As he took all this in, he took another step forward, and suddenly the muffled screams that echoed in the distance magnified. He had been in the city long enough he had forgotten just how loud the choir of anguish that rang out from every point of this place was. He had just barely passed the threshold of the gate and had one foot on the first stair down, but that was enough to leave the muffled quiet of the city and return to the evil loud of the outside.

Josep took another look at the stairs and was doubtful he could even bring himself to traverse them. He had never been particularly afraid of heights in the past, but then again, he had never come so close to a height such as this. The heat from the flames far below began to burn hotter with every second he stood wavering, and he began to step away from the ledge. Something convinced him to turn around before he did, however, and he stopped short, wide-eyed. Less than a foot away stood four of the creatures that had been hunting him through the city. They towered over him and glared down, anxiously waiting for him to return to their domain. The menagerie of horrific skulls included a bird's, a large feline's, something like a bull's, and a human's. Like Josep was staring at the face of death itself, he was transfixed and frozen in fear. Seconds passed without anyone making a move. The creatures didn't seem to need breath, and Josep was holding his.

Josep was certain he was dead—or, whatever it was, he would be if these things had their way with him. He had given thought to whether or not he could in fact die while he was here but had given up trying to figure out the answer without committing to trying it out. He was expecting to find out any second now, but the group just continued to stare at him in silence with their empty, lifeless eyes as if they were waiting on him to make the first move. When he finally realized what was happening, it took him a few moments more to believe it. He looked at his feet and saw that he was past the threshold of the gate, and for some reason, that was important to these monsters.

He looked back up at them, nearly straight up at this angle. For an instant, he considered asking the pack why they would be concerned about something so trivial, but he quickly thought better. He assumed they couldn't or wouldn't talk to him; even if they could, though, he decided he didn't want them to. He looked down at the stairs he now faced and forced himself to squelch the churn in his stomach. Without any other option and wanting to spend as little time in the presence of such hideous beasts, he pressed himself up against the cliff wall as best he could with the intense heat to his back, and he began to very slowly slide down the narrow stairs to whatever terror waited at the bottom.

ELEVEN

As Josep traveled lower, the heat coming up from the fires far below grew hotter and hotter. Yet, somehow, he was also moving farther out from the center of the monstrous stone tree, and so it became darker as he went. An eerie sort of twilight came over Josep's world. Like the sun had hit a ridge at just the right angle, the orange flickering light from below became a deep crimson-red glow. The odd, ashen thunderclouds that had sat above the silent city apparently loomed over the area Josep was approaching as well. For a while, he had been descending between the shadows of the clouds above and the new thunderhead he was delving into. The occasional, distant rolling but muffled sound of thunder was becoming a much more present and booming occurrence. Slight flickers of light far up in the clouds above were now arcing bolts of bright red that shook the ground around him. This was particularly upsetting while he was still high above any sort of solid ground, his face pressed firmly against the fire-baked rock of the stone staircase.

It took him a number of hours zigzagging back and forth across the cliff before he finally began to approach its end. He didn't even finish traversing the stairs; once he had gotten to a distance he felt he could jump, he did just that and rolled as he landed on the gravel path below. It was impossible to see what lay ahead of him when he was above the thick canopy of clouds. Standing below them, now he could see clearly, and he dreaded his next destination.

He was standing on another path very much like the one he traveled just before the silent city. It jutted out of the cliff and led straight toward a massive square structure. At first glance, Josep felt it looked like some sort of fortress or prison. It stood hundreds of feet tall with a sheer rock wall facing him. It was so wide it stretched almost farther than Josep could see in the darkness. There were small windows, but they were far too high up to make out any real detail. Jagged protrusions adorned the top most ridges like a crown of spikes or horns. The only entrance Josep could see was a large square hole at the far side of the path. There was no gate or door, but it was too dark to see what was inside from this distance.

A part of Josep considered stopping at that moment. He had considered giving up numerous times until now, but it was places like this that were truly the only thing resembling reprieve that he had found. The heat was unbearable, the toxic air choked at him every second, he thought he would go mad with thirst, and there was no place he could sit to rest comfortably due to the jagged gravel— and yet, these were the times he wasn't being hunted, imprisoned, or attacked. It was miserable, but it could be worse. He slowly sat himself down in the most comfortable place he could find, which wasn't comfortable in the least, and rested.

There was no chance he could get any real sleep here. But just for a few minutes, he let himself give in to his hesitation. He thought back on everything he had been through so far. Things just kept getting worse the farther he went. He tried to remember the gates of heaven but struggled to remember the exact feeling they filled him with. Even the feeling of real wind was a distant memory now. That was something he had missed far more than he ever would have imagined. The still, stagnant air everywhere he went was gnawing at his soul. What he wouldn't give to be back at those gates now, to feel that magical, wild wind on his face. He rubbed his eyes and unintentionally pressed more sulfurous dust into them while he was trying to clean them out.

Even that hallway would be better than this.

He thought about how foolish he was then, taking hours simply choosing which door to brave. The sound of whatever was banging against the door would be like sweet music compared to the horrific, anguished screams that echoed everywhere he went. His mind noticed the choir of screams anew, and he realized he had all but tuned out for quite a while now. The worst part of it all, though, was that he couldn't quite remember Ashley's face—not the way he wanted to anyways. He would never forget her after the years he'd spent basking in her presence. But it was the little details he cherished so much and that he was so pained to be forgetting now—the little wrinkles by her eyes, the curves that made her ears unique from every other, and the mischievous hairs that broke away from the others and dangled on her face as she slept. He could imagine her smell, but the rancid stench that made his nose burn with every breath he took tore that mental image to shreds and dulled his mind to the clear image he used to have. He had to find her. No matter what he had to endure, he would do it. He wouldn't come all this way just to give up now. All the time he rested, he stared at the door ahead until he had steeled himself yet again. He took a deep breath, fighting back his instinct to gag, and exhaled sharply before pulling himself to his feet. He lied to himself to try and calm his nerves:

After all, how much worse could it be?

He regretted the thought instantly but tried his hardest to force a positive mindset. It had been far too long since he'd had a genuinely happy thought, and it was starting to affect him more and more. There was an end, though. He knew that much. God Himself had told Josep as much when he'd begun this nightmare. If it was possible, then Josep would make it so. He just wished he had some way of knowing how much progress he'd made if any. The not knowing had multiplied each horrific moment such that he had to strain just to remember his life before this place. He knew it was happy; most of it anyway. But individual moments had become harder and harder to recall in any vivid detail. He remembered Ashley, though, and that's all that mattered. He let his mind entertain the notion that she could be in this very building, but that inkling of hope was thrown aside once he approached the gate-like opening.

He was nearly to the other side of the bridge when a scream echoed out louder than the rest that filled the dark sky and drew Josep's gaze toward one of the very high windows. He looked up just in time to see a man throw himself away from the building with all his might. His arms and legs flailing as he went, he fell for a few seconds before he plummeted past the bridge Josep was standing on and down toward the flames far below. His attention was taken away by a guttural laugh, and Josep looked back to where the man had leapt from. It was hard to make out from this distance, but it was hideous and large. Some sort of beast that could just fit its fat arm and gelatinous head out the window was laughing as it watched the man fall. Its body rippled and heaved as it snorted and cackled in delight. It stayed there for only a few seconds more before it slithered back into its hole. Bewildered, Josep's gaze went back over the ledge and found the man. Josep watched as the man fell until he became a squirming silhouette against the intense, bright heat of the flames. After nearly a minute, his form was indistinguishable from the thousands of other bodies that fell, and Josep lost sight of him.

Lost for words, Josep turned again to the massive structure before him. The red lightning streaked across the sky, and for a moment, Josep thought the place to more closely resemble a haunted castle. He had never given any stock to the idea of ghosts, spirits, monsters, or creatures of the night in life. His opinions on the horrors of the world had obviously changed substantially since his death, but even now, he wondered if the idea of vampires and werewolves were something to be concerned with. In life, he felt as if he knew the rules; he knew what to expect when he entered a dark room or went for a midnight stroll in his neighborhood. Here, however, it was like a waking nightmare. Nothing made sense to him, and anytime he felt he had a handle on what might happen next, he found himself very much mistaken. Who was to say whether or not the evil forces that resided in this place couldn't take the form of whatever they wanted? Maybe like a true nightmare, they could become whatever each person dreaded most. Was the experience each poor soul enduring individually tailored to their fears, or was it related to the misdeeds that brought them here in the first place? Surely, they all deserved it for one reason or another. The woman Josep had met in the silent city flashed in his mind again. What did she do to deserve such torment? Josep wanted to believe that she must've been some sort of monster in life and that her monstrous treatment was fitting. He couldn't bring himself to think that, not of her anyways. Her gentle, wounded eyes revealed an innocent soul. But if she was good, then why? Perhaps she was good, but she had not been good enough. How did it all work? If this place was real, which it obviously was, then surely God could not preside over it. Would that not make Him responsible for what went on inside? If it did have its own ruler, was he so concerned with his inhabitants that he'd spend his time on each one, or would he leave that to his subordinates?

Josep forced himself from his pensive state and shook himself awake. None of that mattered right now. Ashley was the goal at hand—as she'd always been—and he would not fail her. He steeled his nerves and finished crossing the last thirty yards of the bridge.

Close enough now to see inside, he wasn't encouraged. The entryway was a very smooth stone of a brighter grayish color than he'd been used to so far, cut into very sharp, square corners. The room stretched back into the darkness with a number of pathways branching this way and that. A stairwell on each side of the room led up to a balcony on the next floor on which he could see even more paths. In seemingly random places, stone sconces were affixed to the walls and emitted a flickering, faint glow of a sickeningly familiar pink hue. This detail put him on edge the most, and without thinking, his heart began to beat much faster and louder than he would've liked.

In the center of the room on a short, square platform was what looked like a large, shallow bowl made of a dark, dented metal. From the entrance, Josep could just make out the light shimmering off some sort of dark liquid inside the bowl. Looking at it altogether, the room felt like the grand foyer to a very unwelcoming mansion. More importantly, though, he didn't detect any signs of life in his immediate vicinity. He wanted it desperately to stay that way. He'd already tried twice to move through the areas he'd been undetected but to no avail. He had no reason to believe this would be any different, but he allowed himself to trust in the old adage: "Third time's the charm." He tentatively took a few steps inside, hugging the wall on his left in the hopes that if anyone did come by, they might pass him without noticing. There were lights all around, but the biggest light source was the light of the flames coming in from outside. The pink sconces cast a very dim light, and most of the interior was decorated with shadows above all else.

There were no immediately obvious signs to distinguish which hall led where, and so he approached the first he came to and cautiously peeked around the corner. A very long and very narrow hallway greeted him. Placed evenly along its length were what looked like stone cell doors. Very narrow slits were carved into some, but not all, of the doors at eye level; but there were no lights inside any of them that he could see. Most concerning was the width of the hall itself, though. There was nowhere to hide if he started down this way; he'd be in the open and easy prey if anything should turn the corner. The pink lights were placed here and there all the way down the hall, and the shadows between them wouldn't be enough to conceal himself completely.

A distant scream echoed down one of the halls on the other side of the foyer. A woman screaming in pain followed closely by a man. It was somewhere way back in the building but was enough to put his nerves on edge all the more. Things had been relatively quiet since he'd entered, but as if the first two screams had set off a chain reaction the entire structure seemed to come alive with tortured shrieks and wails. Looking back down the hall he was closest to, the sounds seemed to be coming out of every cell. Each scream was piercing and filled with an immediate panic and agony. Within the cell closest to Josep was a man's voice. Between his screams were attempts at the words *help* and *no*, but they were cut off each time by more screams.

Within the same cell were the sounds of clambering and commotion and some other sound like a group of animals hissing in anger.

The entire building felt like it was shaking with the cries of collective suffering. Each prisoner's cries reverberated off the stone walls and mingled together to make a single ear-piercing song. It was enough that Josep's hands instinctively went to his ears in an attempt to hide from the sound with little success. He hoped it wouldn't last long but wasn't going to wait and find out.

He followed the wall of the foyer to each passage to see if there were any options that would offer better hiding places should he need one. Unfortunately, though not surprisingly, all of the hallways appeared nearly identical. Long, narrow hallways with short ceilings and dim lighting not only offered little in the way of help, but they also began to feel more and more claustrophobic as Josep inspected them. With his hands still against his ears, he decided to try checking the options on the balcony just in case they led somewhere different. The large alien bowl in the center of the room had drawn his attention more than once, but he had decided it wasn't worth finding out what it was for. It had a strangely foreboding presence, and Josep wasn't anxious to get any nearer. He made his way up the stone steps and realized he couldn't hear his own footsteps. He removed his hands, the screams almost painfully loud now, and confirmed that no noise he could make would break through the cacophony that echoed all around him. He stopped his feet, clapped his hands, and yelled out himself but could hardly distinguish his own scream from the ones around him. This gave him a peculiar sort of comfort to know that he could move about without fear of being heard. He also realized, however, that he'd have to be just as wary of other things moving without his detection.

The noise was too much without some kind of filter, however, and so he planted his fingers back in his ears as best he could. Once he'd reached the top of the stairs, there were two options that looked the same to him. He peeked around the corner to the first hallway and saw a very familiar-looking passage, just like the ones downstairs. Without expecting any change, he moved to the other option, still cautious enough to peek around the edge before relaxing. As the room fell into view, this one was immediately different. Josep's stomach turned at the sight of it before his mind even had time to process exactly what it was.

The dark room had a single iron torch in its center, casting the same sickly pink light. A powerful, gut-wrenching stench slowly filled his lungs. The color splashed against the metal fixtures and sparkled off the pools on the floor. The room was covered in blood and viscera with scarce few places left untouched. After a few moments, Josep even noticed a consistent drip coming from multiple spots on the ceiling. What latched his attention though was the figure hanging aloft near the back wall. Whether it was a man or a woman, Josep honestly couldn't tell. Shackles bolted to the floor, and the ceiling held them a foot off the ground, or rather what remained of them.

There were so many chunks and pieces scattered here and there; bits were even dangling off their form held in place by mere threads of sinew. Josep could only stomach a few seconds of the nauseating sight before his body succumbed. He floundered for a moment in shock before he leaned over the edge of the balcony and retched. During his time here, he'd seen things, horrible things, that turned his stomach and filled him with disgust but nothing quite like this. Whatever had done this didn't do it in a dutiful or meaningful way; even the animal beasts from earlier tore apart their prey with a certain sense of purpose. It was terrible but didn't compare to this unrivaled display of sadism. There was nothing in his stomach to relieve himself of, but his body reacted just the same.

His cracked lips and dry throat burned on contact with what little did exit his mouth. When he had stopped his dry heaving, his morbid curiosity got the better of him, and he dared one last glance to confirm it was real. There were any number of jagged metal blades and devices strewn across the floor of the chamber, and all of them looked as if they had seen great use. A single drain in the corner of the room kept the veritable river of body fluids from spilling out into the foyer, despite the fact it looked like it was nearly completely blocked by aging remains.

Josep turned away quickly when he felt his stomach reacting again. Was this what all the voices screaming around him were suffering now? This was beyond terrible, and now the choir of pain seemed that much louder in his mind. His hands went back to his ears to try and stop it, but the screams were too loud. This was a new kind of nightmare, one beyond what he'd experienced so far. Before, he had been scared, terrified even. Now he was absolutely petrified. He was trembling with fear, and a cold sweat had already begun to drench his filthy clothes. His heart was fluttering in his chest like it was about to explode, and he felt lightheaded. There were sparkles in his vision, and he felt like he was suffocating. The idea of suffering something like that forever was too much to handle. There had to be some other way around this place; getting caught before meant suffering and torment, but this was too much.

There was nowhere to go; he knew that. But he had to get out of this place now regardless. He scrambled to his feet and began to rush toward the stairs back down until he caught something out of the corner of his eye. A lumbering shadow was shifting along the walls coming from one of the hallways he'd checked earlier. In a panic, he backed up and positioned himself on the threshold of the passage, away from the torture room. His eyes went back and forth between the shadow and the exit. He could see the bridge and the base of the cliff far away from this place. It didn't matter if he had to backtrack all the way to the coliseum; he'd find another way to get to wherever he was going.

The shadow shifted a few seconds more before its source came into view. A monster squeezed its way through the narrow passage and into the foyer. It stood a head taller than Josep but was much, much larger. Thick folds of skin hung over each other and swung back and forth as it waddled. It was adorned in large metal piercings of all different shapes including hooks, rods, and studs of varying sizes. The creature's noxious pale skin was covered in massive warts and oozing pustules from horned head to stubby toe. It didn't seem to have any real neck as its wide, toothy grin seemed to grow out of its rotund body and sit below a large number of beady black eyes. An odd number of misshapen horns sat like a deformed crown atop the beast. It dragged one of its trunk-like legs behind itself as it shuffled toward the stairs. All the while, it twiddled its fingers in the air like a child about to rip into a present on Christmas morning. Was this the thing that had viscously torn apart the remains next door? The possibility of that being true and of running into it refilled Josep's deepest parts with a terror, unlike anything he'd experienced. Before he knew it, he was sprinting down the hall as fast as he could, with no idea where he was going, the screams all around leading him on.

He ran the length of the passageway until he came to its end. Two branches broke off in opposite directions, each looking very much the same. Without any consideration, he dashed to his right and continued deeper into the prison. At the end of that hall, he turned again, and again, and again. At some point, he turned a corner and found a set of stairs leading down to a lower floor. He took them two at a time without hesitation, hoping for some way out. To his dismay, the lower level was much like the upper. Each hall was roughly a hundred yards long and had randomly placed pink sconces throughout. All of the cells lining the walls played their own unique melody of torment. Without paying much attention, he'd heard the sounds of rushing water, roaring fires, animal roaring and hissing and biting, insects swarming, electrical arcing, and machinery grinding. Every cell seemed to contain its own specific form of torture, and a single screaming voice came out of each and mingled with the others.

Josep ran for quite a long while before he was exhausted, and his body forced him to come to a stop. After traversing more than a dozen halls and multiple stairways, he doubled over, lungs burning, and gasped for air. Beads of sweat dripped off his face and splashed against the brick floor. Somewhere along the way, while his mind was consumed with his desire to get away, he'd moved to some part of the prison where the dull gray stone was replaced with murky yellowish brickwork. Everything else was the same, though. Long, cramped hallways lined with torture cells led this way and that without any sort of indication as to what belonged where. He took a few moments to catch his breath, his hands still covering his ears as they had been this whole time. There was no break in the anguished song. Josep wondered if it was possible for any of the people here to pass out; surely by now, had they been alive, they all would've succumbed to their suffering and either died or at least fallen unconscious. As if being fueled by some otherworldly force, however, the screams continued to ring out without reprieve. Josep had grown somewhat accustomed to the sounds of pain during his time traveling the outside, but here, the sounds were so much more acute. They dug into his ears and clawed at his mind. Someone had to help these people. How could anyone endure this for so long?

He chose a cell closest to him as his breathing returned to normal. The voice inside was a woman's, and the accompanying noise sounded something like a power saw. The slit in the door was barely enough to see through, and the room inside was far too dark to make anything out. He inspected the door for some way to open it. The door was flush with the wall around it, leaving only a thin crack to indicate it was a door at all. There were no handles or visible locks he could find, only an oddly shaped hole near the center of the door he assumed was for a key. All of the doors were like this; the only difference was that some doors were without any slit at all. Try as he might, he had very few options, and nothing seemed effective in the slightest. Unless he could find the key, he'd have no chance at opening any of these doors.

His senses returned now; he looked down both directions and realized something he had been too afraid to consider before: He had no idea where he was. In his panicked state at the sight of the lumbering creature, he'd lost all sense of direction and had simply been running on instinct. Something else he hadn't considered until now was the likelihood that there were more than one of the monsters roaming the halls.

He'd been a fool, blinded by his fear. This place got to him more than the rest he'd been to. Josep had felt dread, hopelessness, despair, and fear; but this place filled him with a uniquely targeted sense of uncontrollable terror. Perhaps his spirits had been broken down over time, or maybe this place drew on something more primal than what he'd seen before. Either way, he'd gotten himself into a particularly bad situation now, and didn't know what to do about it. He abandoned hope of returning to the entrance; after all, even if he did make it back, he had nowhere to go unless he was willing to return to the coliseum and he knew that journey would be absolute folly. There had to be some sort of exit and that was his new goal. He continued to the end of this hall, being level-headed enough now to peek around the corner first, and then started down the next.

Josep turned a few more corners without any change, wondering if he was doomed to repeat his aimless wandering in the tunnels before when something did happen. All at once, with only a few seconds of transition in between, the screaming stopped. Every voice, every sound accompanying them, the choir of anguished pain just stopped. The change was so stark and so sudden that Josep panicked for a moment, thinking something had happened to his hearing. He removed his hands from his ears, and the silence was all the more deafening. Too scared to say anything, he snapped his fingers to confirm he could still hear. He looked about, terribly confused, but nothing else happened. As if on a schedule, just as suddenly as the screaming had begun, it simply ended. Standing still for a moment, with no change, he moved to a cell nearby and pressed his ear against the slit. Ever so faintly, he could hear a voice. There were no words, only faint, spastic breathing in the darkness. Josep's only guess was that once the allotted time was over, the torment abruptly ended, and everyone passed out just as quickly. He whispered into the cell, "Hello?"

He tried a number of times on a number of different cells but with no response. Some cells were completely silent; others had the same sort of irregular breathing. None of them held any conscious prisoners, or if they did, they were far too weak to answer. Undoubtedly, anyone who survived such a long, ceaseless agony had to have their spirits broken at the very least. Perhaps even their minds had come undone? Josep wondered for himself how he could possibly cope under such circumstances. How could one stay sane under these conditions, over and over, with no end in sight? Could there be anything worse than an eternal agony with absolutely no hope of rescue? That was the thing he had to hold tight: hope. The voice he'd heard when this all began promised a possibility of returning with Ashley. As long as there was a chance, that was all he needed. With that, he could continue. And so like a steadfast rock in an ever more intense and violent sea, he latched onto it with all his might. Ashley was here somewhere. He had to be getting close.

Now that the sounds of the prisoners had ceased, he was far more conscientious of his movements. It was easy enough to conceal the sound of his footprints and breathing, but it was one more thing to add to his list of concerns. He was lucid for now, but the thought of running into another one of those sickening abominations in these tight, restrictive hallways kept his pulse at an alarming rate. He wiped at the sweat that threatened to fall into his eyes and continued on.

Shortly after, only a few halls later, he peeked around the next corner and found another change. At this intersection, the hall to his right was another hall like the rest, but the passage to his left led to another room like the one he'd seen before. A dimly lit chamber was filled with jagged blades and horrible devices for inflicting pain. Near the back wall was another figure, held aloft by iron shackles attached to the ceiling and floor. At first glance, he thought he would have to turn away in disgust again. The room was plastered with blood and human remains, and the odor was unbearable, but the nude figure seemed to be intact. After a moment of observation, he seemed to move. The man's head was hung low, his body limp and emaciated. He was bruised and scarred all over, but he had not been torn into the same way as the body from before. Josep checked the corners to ensure they were alone before he hazarded a sound, "Psst!"

The man reacted immediately. He jerked to life as if he'd been asleep and then raised his head to meet Josep's gaze. The man had a ragged, full beard. His dark hair hung over his eyes, and he had to cock his head to see clearly. The man, like all the others Josep had seen so far, seemed to be in his thirties and would've been considered quite fit had he not been so abused and malnourished. His eyes went wide, and he sprung to life as best he could. The man tried to speak but gagged and had to clear his throat to make any kind of human sound. He spat some sort of dark fluid on the floor before he managed to communicate clearly. His voice was burly and, to Josep, didn't seem to fit his frame at all, "Help! Get me down! Please! I'm begging you! It'll be back soon!"

Josep turned around quickly to check behind. He hadn't heard any noise to indicate something was approaching, but knowing one had been here earlier set him on edge all the more. He turned back to the chained man. "That creature?"

"Yes! One of them. They're all over the place. Just get me down! We'll get out of here. Just don't leave me! Please!" The man spoke in a hushed tone but with a panicked urgency.

Josep was reluctant to trust some stranger he knew nothing about, but he had been lacking a companion for so long now. He had no idea where he was or how to escape, but if this man could help, then maybe they would both have a chance. Josep cautiously moved a few steps closer. "Do you know how to get out?"

Without hesitation, the man shot back, "Yes, yes, yes! Just get me down! I can't take this anymore, just get me free!"

Josep paused for just a moment before he decided to give the man a chance. If the man was telling the truth, he would need his help. Josep inspected the shackles around the man's feet. They were made of iron but were too small for the man's legs. They had dug into his skin, and after wearing them as long as he had, massive bloodied welts had formed all around. Josep also saw that each shackle had a keyhole. "Where're the keys?"

"Somewhere in here," the man responded. "They all use the same one. That thing leaves it in here to taunt me. He just tossed it in the corner somewhere, I don't know!"

Josep squinted in the dim lighting and crouched to try and scan the room. The bloodied remains of prior victims were piled up without rhyme or reason. The metal tools that were strewn about the place made it even more of a mess to decipher. Josep was reluctant to go digging through any piles at first but knew he had to hurry or risk being captured himself. He held his breath, despite knowing it wouldn't help in the least, and dug his hands into the nearest pile that might be hiding the key. He wriggled his fingers in the filth for a few seconds before moving to the next pile. His body had to be positioned to not block what little light was cast by the pink torch in the center of the room, but it didn't help much either way. To his disgust, he had to rely on his sense of touch far more than his sight.

He reached into another pile and cut his hand on something sharp. He reeled back and kicked at the pile revealing some sort of bladed instrument hiding under the guts. He only inspected the wound for an instant before conceding that he had no way to distinguish his own blood from the rest that now coated his hands and most of his forearms. He pulled bones and organs aside as he continued to dig through the room's contents. The chained man grew more frantic with each moment. "Come on! Hurry it up! It could be back any minute now! They come back when the screaming stops so they can hear me better, the bastards."

Josep sped up, but only a bit. He had to be methodical or risk spending far more time searching. He started in another pile in one of the darker corners before asking, "How do we get out of here?"

"Oh, no, no, no. I'll show you when I'm out of this. You're not leaving me here. I'm not staying in this god-forsaken place any longer. I'm getting the f—"

Josep cut the man off as soon as he was sure, "I got it!"

He wiped off some of the grime that was sticking to the metal key he now held as he walked back toward the man. The chained man was ecstatic. "Good! Good! Good! Good! Now get me out of these things! Quick!"

It was a very strangely shaped key. When he'd first grabbed it, he almost discarded it as some bizarre torture device. It was thick and had a handle like what he expected, but the key itself was in an odd, twisted shape, resembling a corkscrew. He fumbled to fit it into the lock and failed more than once.

The man clamored impatiently, "Hurry up!"

Finally, the key slipped into place and seemed to twist itself. The lock snapped open, and one chain fell to the floor, splattering and clanging as it did.

"Shhh!" The man exclaimed in a panic, "Are you trying to screw us over?"

Josep moved quickly to the other leg and released it as well, this time catching the shackle and lowering it without much noise. He then stretched to reach high enough to unlock the man's hands, but it was just above his reach. Josep spun around to find something to stand on, his toes squishing in the muck. It didn't need to be much, just a few inches. He spotted something laying on the ground behind where the man was hanging; it looked like some sort of metal wheel with raised studs and curled hooks. The important thing was that it had some sort of squared frame where the handles were attached. He grabbed it and positioned it by the man's dangling feet. The man continued to badger Josep to move faster every step of the way. He could finally step up just enough to reach the locks. The device was uneven and wobbled as he tried to keep his balance without standing on the razor-like protrusions. One lock came undone and the man's arm immediately dropped to his side. Dangling now by one hand, he began to swing back and forth. Josep caught his arm and stood on his toes to finish the job. As the lock snapped open, the man fell to the ground like a brick and now lay in a heap in the grime. Josep hopped down from his perch and went to help the man to his feet. The man was alert, though, and was already pulling himself up. His arms were limp at his sides, and he struggled to get his feet under himself. Before Josep could do anything to help, the man protested, "No, no. I got it. Let's go!"

Like a newborn trying to keep upright, the man struggled to stand straight. He settled by stumbling through the viscera until he met with the wall by the door and pushed himself to his feet. He swore as he realized he wouldn't be able to use his arms. It was easy enough to see now that he stood in front of Josep; the man's shoulders were dislocated at the very least. Unnatural lumps seemed to show that many of the man's bones weren't at all where they were meant to be. Along with that, burn marks, open holes, and gaping cuts covered the man all over. He nearly toppled over as he leaned to look down the hall Josep had come from.

Josep began to ask but was cut off, "Are you sure you're al—"

"Shut up! I'll manage until I'm out of here." The man righted himself again and checked down both corridors.

Josep conceded to let the man handle himself. There wasn't anything he could do for him now anyways. He focused on the task at hand. "So how do we get out of here?"

Without looking back, keeping a frantic watch out for any movement, "I heard if we get down to the bottom of the prison, there's an exit. Some guy got out a long time ago down there." Once he was sure the coast was clear, he pushed against the wall to get started and shambled down the hall.

"Someone else escaped?" Josep asked.

"Yeah, apparently. I've never seen him, but I've heard people talk about him; some idiot who got himself out just to get stuck back here again. That's not gonna be me. I'm getting out of here for good."

The two of them made it to the end of the hall, checked to make sure it was clear, and continued down the next. Their voices were lowered, but the possibility of escape made speed the higher priority. The cells they passed seemed to Josep more akin to graves without the sound of screaming. Josep asked, "How long until they start screaming again?"

Without breaking his hobbling stride, "A while. The torture isn't as fun for the jailers if we don't have the energy to scream. That was a shorter session, so it might be sooner than later, but we should be out of here by then."

Josep tried not to think about it too much, but the thought forced its way in: If that was a "shorter session," what must the long ones be like? He didn't have an accurate read on how long it had gone on. Honestly, since his time in the tunnels, his sense of time had been all but destroyed. At a blind estimate, he assumed it had to have been nearly two hours of relentless screaming, though. His body didn't work the same as it had in life, that much was obvious, but could a human—in anybody—truly take such ruthless torment? How long could one's mind possibly last under such conditions? Surely, at some point, their grip on reality would crumble to dust if it hadn't already. At a certain point, would they even be considered human, or would they eventually turn to empty shells? For some reason, Josep's mind had been asking more and more of these kinds of questions, and he didn't like it. He'd always been a thinker, or at least thought of himself as one. The macabre tone his thoughts had been taking concerned him, though, and he tried his best to push them down. He needed his mind focused on his current situation. Escape first, then on to Ashley. This threw a new idea to the forefront and nearly stopped him in his tracks as it did. Was Ashley a prisoner here? It was possible, wasn't it? Then again, she could've been in any of the places he'd been so far. This had been his problem all along: not knowing where the end goal was or how to get there.

When he'd first begun this journey, the creature in the coliseum told him to follow his instincts, and he'd end up in the right place. Josep hardly trusted the word of something that called this place its home, but he had no other choice. Now he had a new source of information, and so as they continued to navigate the long, cramped corridors. He asked another question, "I've been looking for my wife. Do you know a woman named Ashley here?"

The man scoffed. "What the hell do I look like to you? No, I don't know anyone's name here, and I don't care either. I have my own problems to deal with, and I'm not looking to take on anyone else's. You wanna wander this place on your own? Knock yourself out, but I'm getting the hell out of here."

It wasn't the answer Josep was looking for, but it honestly didn't surprise him. The man was helping Josep escape the worst place he'd been in so far, but Josep didn't like him. It was more than just the fact that he was rude. Josep could forgive that given the man's circumstances. Josep thought for sure that if they'd met in life, at some restaurant or at the grocery store, the man would've been just as cordial as anyone else you'd meet. That's what he told himself anyways. There was something else about him. Something Josep hadn't put his finger on, but it made him far more wary than he wanted to be. He didn't suspect the man to be lying, only that he was out for his own interests above all else. Then again, who knew how long he'd been here? Josep's priority would have been to escape at all costs as well, had their positions been swapped, right? He was thinking too much into it, surely. Again, he tried to suppress the distracting thoughts that swirled in his mind, but this one kept gnawing at him.

Josep resigned to escape this place and figure things out from there. It's what he'd been doing so far, and he had to trust that it would somehow work out in the end. Eventually, the road he'd been traveling had to come to some sort of final destination. When it did, if he still hadn't found Ashley, he would turn right around and come back the way he came. He had a goal, and time was something he had plenty of now. Granted he'd much rather be spending it anywhere but here, but once he saved the love of his life, he'd take her home, and they'd make up for it together.

The two came to another intersection, and after peeking, the corner followed another stairwell down. They'd followed a number of these stairs down now. So far, the man had been traveling the halls like he knew every twist and turn, but Josep was completely lost. Everywhere looked the same. The cells were all identical. There were no distinctive features to any of the halls, aside from the occasional splatter or trail of blood that led to and from certain cells. The stairwells were all simple single-flights that led directly from one floor to the floor below. Everywhere was dimly lit with the same ominous pink light. The fortunate thing was that, so far, they hadn't run into any guards, nor had they heard any threatening sounds.

After a few more steps, that changed. It was far off in the distance, but it was coming from the direction they were heading. It was too garbled at first, but after continuing a bit more at a much slower pace, it began to clear. The sound was something like laughter, but deep, disgusting, and painful. To Josep, it sounded less like a real laugh and more like rocks in a blender. Without seeing anything, it was clear the source was something foul and deformed, but it cackled with childish glee. The other sound with it was a pounding, squelching sound Josep hesitated to identify. The man leading Josep knew straight away what it was. He turned to Josep and whispered, almost inaudibly, "We have to sneak by. The stairs are down this hall."

Josep was terrified. He'd been grateful at their luck so far, but the moment he'd been dreading was approaching. The two moved far more slowly and far more quietly than they had been, but they moved with purpose as fast as they could manage. The man had stumbled every so often as they had been wandering, but he was far more deliberate now. It was obvious he had no intention of making a mistake here. They approached the end of the hall, turned the corner, and slowly traveled the next. The sound grew louder with each step until it was finally just around the corner. At this distance, the noises were far clearer and more graphic than Josep would have ever wanted. The room to their left was another chamber like the one

Josep had rescued the man from. It was easy enough to imagine what was going on inside. Despite his best attempts not to, Josep's mind did just that. The creature's weight was obvious by its heavy footfalls. Each step was a mixture of squelching splashes in the pool it stood in, and the occasional pop of bones snapping under its girth. The monster would step this way and that, chortling and giggling to itself. Its laughter could hardly be called so, mucus and phlegm choked at every sound, but the thing was far too enamored with its work to care about clearing its throat. And then, after dancing this way and that, the beast paused to reel back and hack away at its victim. There were no screams of pain, or any human sounds at all, just the splatter of flesh that came with each swing.

The two were standing just around the corner, pressed tight up against the wall. The man was closest to the corner and moved at a snail's pace as he peeked around to see the room. Josep couldn't see inside, and he didn't intend to. He waited for the man to give him the signal it was okay to move. They needed to travel the hall to their right, and hopefully, they could make it to the end without the monster noticing. It was a disgusting thought, but Josep hoped the monster would be too distracted by its current activity to notice the two of them at all. He tried not to imagine any images at all, but the sounds told a story all too clearly, and flashes of the room he'd seen before came as fast as he could send them away.

Seconds went by as Josep waited. He focused on keeping his breathing as quiet as he could, but his heart was pounding louder and louder in his chest, and his breathing quickened with it. A bead of sweat slowly ran down his face as he stared unblinking, waiting for the signal to move. The man was standing, or rather slouching, with his back against the wall. His arms still hung limp at his sides. Josep tried not to stare at the gouges and wounds all over his body, but he wondered just how long the man had been here. He seemed to imply that he was relatively new to this place, but he knew the prison so well he must've been here for quite a long time. There was certainly no reason for him to lie, none that Josep could tell. Then again, Josep also had no idea how his new body would react to such prolonged torture. Maybe the man had been hacked to pieces himself in the past, and somehow his body had healed? If they died, did they awake with new bodies like nothing had ever happened, doomed to repeat the cycle again and again? This place was getting to him, clearly. He wasn't usually this grim. But it didn't really matter anyway; Josep wasn't going to stay long enough to find out.

A few seconds more passed, though it felt much longer, before the man silently pushed himself off the wall and quickly tiptoed toward the hall on their right, away from the sounds they'd been listening to. Josep followed close behind. The creature seemed to be making enough noise it wouldn't notice the slight pitter-patter of their feet on the stone, but they weren't going to take any chances. Taking long strides, they rushed down the hall. It was just like any of the others but somehow felt much longer. The hundred yards or so to the end felt more like a hundred miles. The light was dim, and shadows followed them everywhere; but if the beast looked down the hall even for a moment, they would without a doubt be seen.

In these moments, the sounds of horror behind them were a good thing; it meant they were still unseen. The beast continued to chortle and snort to itself as it played with its toy. Squishing in the gore. A pause as it readied itself for another swing. Cracking and tearing of meat. A maniacal gurgling. Another pause, and then more splashing steps as it danced around. Josep hadn't seen, but it could only be a human victim the monster was tormenting, right? He dared not take a look back, but there hadn't been any human sounds since they first approached. Surely anyone would be long dead by now. What was the creature doing? Hacking away at a lump of flesh? Josep wondered if it had a will of its own at all. Did it function like a machine, mindlessly laboring away at a task that was assigned to it? Was it like a wild beast, autonomous but without any self-awareness or higher intelligence? Or could it be it was just as alive as Josep was, and it simply enjoyed the suffering of others without end?

The two of them were halfway down the hall. They stepped as quickly as they could, making sure to move silently above all else. Josep was hunched over, nearly crouching as he ran. It wouldn't help any, but it made him feel safer. The sounds behind them were slowly fading but not fast enough. The beast was still distracted, though.

They were going to make it. Closer now. The creature was too enthralled and hadn't even considered looking away from its prey. They were near the end. In seconds, they would turn the corner and be out of sight. A part of Josep was curious to look behind, but he dared not. His curiosity had nearly cost him too many times already. He would tame it this time. Thirty feet now. The tension in Josep's chest was building, and he was ever more anxious for it to release.

Suddenly, a noise exploded all around and filled the halls all at once. It came from everywhere. Josep stuttered for a moment, but the man ahead broke into a sprint. Josep forced himself forward as he was still realizing what it was. A beast, very similar sounding to the one they were escaping, was growling something loud like an announcer over a loudspeaker, though from where Josep couldn't tell. Its voice was a mixture of phlegm and gravel, but piercing notes mingled at random. It was gurgling its words more than speaking them, "The rat's back in the maze!" It roared with an undeniable glee. The words were human—and English—but the beast spoke them like someone who knew their sound, not their meaning. It followed the words with something that sounded far more familiar to its tongue. This sound also resembled words, but of an alien and evil origin that Josep's mind wouldn't dare to try and decipher.

Immediately, the sounds of distracted glee behind the two ceased. As the voice that rang out through the halls disappeared, a new noise took its place. The man in front of Josep had turned the corner, and Josep was right on his heels. As he rounded the corner, he instinctively took a momentary glance down the way they had come. For an instant, his eyes met the monster's. As soon as he saw the deformed, hulking beast, he was out of sight. But it was too late. Josep sprinted after the man, all semblance of stealth abandoned, as a roar echoed out down the hall. They'd been seen.

The man leading Josep let loose a slew of curses. His arms dangled behind him as he began to run far faster than Josep expected him capable of. "Dammit! I'm not getting caught! I'm not staying here anymore!"

Josep pushed himself harder to keep pace. He was beginning to panic but fought to keep his wits. Surely, the monstrous, rotund thing he'd seen behind was incapable of moving anywhere near fast enough to keep up with their mad dash. He wouldn't risk testing that, of course, but they were too far ahead now for it to matter, right? Josep turned his gaze back as he ran. He saw no beast, just the empty hall that led back into darkness too far to see. They were fine. Home free, even. He looked ahead again. The man was somehow moving faster than he could keep up, so Josep redoubled his efforts.

They turned another corner to a set of stairs. The man ahead barely touched them at all, leaping the last half and tumbling when he landed. Josep nearly fell as he took them two at a time. He hadn't even made it halfway down before the man had returned to his feet and continued his escape. The man obviously wouldn't be waiting for Josep, and so Josep refused to lose him. They continued to run, down one hall, then another, and another. Both the men were huffing, lungs on fire. Nothing had caught them yet, though. In fact, Josep hadn't seen or heard anything since the roar from before. However, no sooner could the thought flutter through his mind did a sound emerge from the depths of the prison. At first, it was indecipherable, a loud, unspecified rumbling that came from both in front and behind. It took only moments before it was much louder, though. To Josep, it sounded like a herd of pigs, snorting and grunting, until he heard the rhythm of laughter. It must have been a horde of the creatures coming from every direction.

When the two made it to a new hallway, Josep was bewildered that he still had no clue where it was coming from. The swarm was giving chase, but the two were also running toward them. They were everywhere. Josep's head was on a swivel, looking back every few seconds and glancing down every hall they turned away from. He hadn't seen any of the beasts, but the sound was too loud for them to be far away. It sounded like at any moment they would turn the corner, and it would all be over. Another stairway came, and the two flew down it as fast as before. It wasn't much longer though before their bodies began to give out. The man ahead was still keeping an impressive pace, but he had slowed, and he stumbled with every few strides. Both the men heaved with each painful gasp of air.

It couldn't be much farther, could it? Josep had long ago lost count of how many floors they had traveled, but they had been running for miles, and that was after traveling miles more undetected. The structure was monumental, far larger than anything that could exist in the living world, but everything had to have an ending at some point, right? Just as Josep was beginning to doubt if that was true, to Josep's surprise, the man ahead of him spoke. Still forcing his body forward with all his waning might, huffing between each word, "It's…so…close…just…one…more…floor!"

Could it be so? A twinge of much-needed hope flickered in Josep's spirit. They were going to make it. Of course, they were. The voice said it could be done when Josep started. How could he have ever doubted? The cackling herd of gurgling voices was louder than ever now, but he still hadn't seen a thing. As the two approached the next turn, Josep took yet another glance behind, and his heart sunk. This time, he saw the monsters clearer than ever. A flood of the things filled the hall in a stampede of bodies. They were turning the corner at the other end of the hall but were running far faster than Josep had expected. The horde lurched and jerked as they threw their heaving, gelatinous bodies toward their prey. More than once, they jumped over the one in front and trampled one another without mercy. The hall was filled to the brim with rotting flesh, and the stream was flowing directly toward Josep. Suddenly, a burst of adrenaline filled Josep more than ever before, and he sprang back to full speed. He would've screamed had he not been so afraid. All of the images and sounds of his time in this place filled his mind and flashed before his eyes. He wouldn't get stuck here. He couldn't. Ashley's face joined the parade of images. His heart skipped a beat. She hadn't been so clear since he'd seen her last. This wasn't the end. He wouldn't let it be. He was destined to find her, and they were going to escape.

Josep slid around the corner and nearly crashed into the man ahead of him. He'd stopped. Josep nearly screamed in terror and confusion until he looked down the hall to what the man was staring at, and he too froze in fear. At the far end of this hall was another beast, this one larger than all the others. Its crown of horns was far taller and more mangled than the rest. Spikes jutted out of its thick, bare hide along with random bits of metal and piercings. Its skin was mottled, and instead of a rotten pale, it was a searing, violent red.

Josep wanted to run. He wanted to scream, but the same thing that froze the man with him froze Josep: The beast didn't see them. Its back was turned to them, and it was looking down the next two halls, trying to decide where to turn next. Did it not hear the cacophony behind it, or did it assume the horde behind him was still searching too? In either case, the two men had no options. This was the way to go, according to the man. But the river of death was fast approaching behind them.

Seconds passed like hours as they stood transfixed on the red monster's every movement. It looked this way and that until it finally decided which way it would go, and it lumbered down the hall to its left. The two stood still for only a second more and then sprang back to life. They had no other choice but to move forward. They sprinted as fast as their legs would carry them. They made it halfway down the hall before the river spilled into view behind. The chortling and laughing had devolved into an even more erratic shrieking now. With their targets so close, their excitement had reached a fever pitch. Death was seconds away, but they could still make it.

They reached the end of the hall, and the man ahead of Josep dashed to the right. Without looking, Josep moved to follow when a massive arm moved like a snake striking its target. Faster than Josep's eye could comprehend, the man ahead of him had been snatched and yanked to Josep's left. He couldn't skip a beat; his body was moving on its own now. He jerked forward and started down the hall on his right, but his head turned to his left as he did. The massive red monster had been hiding just around the corner, waiting for them to pass. This close, Josep could see it clearly now. It had to bend over ever so slightly to fit in the shallow passageway. Its horns scraped the ceiling as it moved. Its vibrant red skin was, in fact, a thick coat of blood. Older coatings of dried blood had turned black, but fresh, wet crimson ran down its body and splashed on the floor as it moved. In its massive left hand, it carried a massive crooked blade covered in as much blood as the rest of the brute. And now in its right claw, it held aloft the man who had been leading Josep this far. Innumerable black teeth escaped its maw as a monstrous grin stretched far wider than any living creature Josep had seen before. Two small, glossy black beads sat planted above its smile. Like a shark, it seemed to be looking nowhere and everywhere all at once, but Josep could feel the creature's hot gaze, and he was reminded of the creature at the coliseum.

His back rapidly began to heat up as he turned to face the new hall he'd entered. A roar, louder, more monstrous, and more elated than anything else he'd heard shook the world around Josep. Tears burst forth as Josep couldn't contain the animalistic terror he now felt. He let out a scream that came from a deeper, more honest place than he knew he had. It seemed the stones beneath his feet would shatter as the beast behind him let out a belly laugh. The man he was holding screamed in a terror of his own, flailing aimlessly as he did. The beast then let out words between its cackles, "Simon! Where do you think you're going? We haven't even started to have fun with you yet!" The beast laughed manically as Josep twisted to see.

Just as things came into view, through his tear-blurred vision, Josep watched as the monster threw the man down the hall they'd come from. The man's shrill screaming and curses disappeared in a storm of howling and cackling horrors. There was no hope for him now. His screams followed Josep down the hall, but soon, the sounds of the monsters tearing him apart quickly drowned them out. The massive red monster focused its gaze on Josep, and the heat felt like it would roast him on the spot. The bloody jailer began to dash forward and scraped at the stone as it forced its massive frame through the narrow corridor. The prison walls cracked, and the floors trembled as it bounded toward Josep like a rabid animal. Sweat poured off Josep, leaving a trail as he screamed and flailed his arms, hoping without reason that it would make him move faster. His mind was a senseless blur; had the bloody jailer's booming voice not been so painfully loud, Josep would not have heard its taunt.

"Where are you going? It's been so long since I've had any real fun! The maggots I toy with bore me to tears. I want some real fun!" The creature was ecstatic, rapturous even. Unbridled joy dripped off every word it vomited out.

Josep was in a primal state now. His heart felt like it would explode at any moment. His head was pounding and spinning, and the room around him swirled. His vision was blurring at the edges as he sprinted and screamed at no one in particular. At the end of the hall, he turned on instinct, with no consideration at all for where he might end up. He turned this way and that. All the while, the beast tore through the prison getting closer and closer as they ran. Josep wasn't listening. He wasn't in any state of mind to think rationally, but he did hear the creature as its cries grew louder. "Get back here! You're mine, Josep! I want to taste your meat! Meat! I want my play-time, Josep! You can't get away from me! You're mine! Mine! Mine!"

Josep's mind was a total blur. He turned another corner and didn't even take time to process the new room he'd entered. The hall he was in opened up into a still small but larger chamber than the ones he was used to. On the far side was another hallway, and with-out skipping a beat, he ran right for it. The raving monster was upon him. Less than a second after Josep entered the room, the mad beast did also. Josep could feel his presence. He'd be snatched up within seconds. Then suddenly, the world fell away. A blast of wind shot up from below, and the world went dark. He was still awake and flailing wildly. It took him a few moments to realize he'd fallen. He looked up at the rapidly fleeing roars of the beast. Blasphemies and curses spewed forth from its furious maw. Its arm was reaching down the hole, but Josep was far too gone for it to pose any threat. The rush of the chase was replaced by the rush of falling.

It had been nearly ten seconds now. He was in total blackness. The air was far colder now than it had been. The dim pink light and the roars of the monster were both tiny specks far above. Was this the end? Had he simply tripped into oblivion? Did his journey end so abruptly in failure? He couldn't see anything. His own screams echoed out in the void without reply. His vision was filled with inky black. And then, just as suddenly as the ground had disappeared, so did his senses. A split second of impact and his mind went blank.

TWELVE

"Well, it was very nice to meet you both."

"Same to you!"

"And I hope we'll get to see you both Thursday night."

"Yes, we appreciate the invite! We'll be looking forward to it. Thank you!"

"Of course. Have a blessed day, you two!"

Ashley was so good at this sort of thing it blew Josep away. Within five minutes, she could talk to a complete stranger like they'd known each other their entire lives. Josep wasn't that way at all. He didn't mind the socializing, but it took him a good bit longer to decide whose company he enjoyed and how to approach them. Somehow, though, she could always jump right in. Josep smiled and waved briefly at the couple as he turned to leave. Ashley took a few moments more to exchange pleasantries before she turned away. She pulled her phone out of her purse to make a note right away; she'd made it a habit to put reminders about all her plans someplace she wouldn't forget. Josep stared enraptured at her lips as she silently mumbled the words in her head. They were heading toward their car, but until she finished typing, she was essentially at a standstill. She moved in slow motion, and, to Josep, so did the rest of the world. The golden sunlight danced around her like a shining goddess. How did he get so lucky? She finished her typing and returned to the world. A wide smile plastered across her face until she saw his.

Her cheeks blushed. "What?"

Josep answered automatically, still lost in her beauty, "What what?"

"Stop staring!" She sheepishly walked, or rather skipped, to catch up to her husband. Her arm slipped around his, and she gave him a giddy, if slightly embarrassed, grin.

Josep shook himself awake. "Was I?"

"Yes! You do it all the time!"

"Well, can I help it if you're fun to stare at?"

She played at being against the idea. "Well, now you're making it sound like I'm some kind of circus attraction?"

Without skipping a step, "Do circuses have angels as attractions?"

Her cheeks were nearly beet red now, and she quickly changed the subject. She broke eye contact to help herself cool off. "So what do think about them?"

Josep was still enjoying the view but allowed her evasion. "I mean, they seem nice."

"No, I mean about their invitation. It sounds like a good chance to get more involved in the church, to meet more people."

Josep wasn't particularly eager to spend an evening with the new couple they'd met. He wasn't particularly eager to socialize with any of the people at this church. He knew that Ashley enjoyed the social-izing and the atmosphere, though, so he didn't mind as long as he was with her. Josep answered, "Yeah, it sounds all right. Might be fun."

Ashley read through his bluff immediately. "You don't like them?"

"No, no. I don't mean it like that. They seem nice." Before Ashley could prod further, he continued, "There aren't really a lot of couples our age here, though, right? I dunno. I mean, it's not that I don't want to, but we just spent the night with Jordan and Shirley last night."

"Well, I know, but it came up when I was talking about our family, and how we were looking to meet people in our church." She hesitated a moment, and Josep knew there was something else. "And, well, I was hoping maybe your parents would want to join us some time if we thought they were nice."

Josep held back a scoff, "Baby, come on. We've talked about this a million times."

Ashley began to fiddle with her nails as she spoke, "Well, yeah, I know. But it's been a while since we brought it up, and I just thought—"

"Baby, I love you. And I know you just want to get us all closer, but my parents aren't interested in this kind of thing. We've invited them before—more than once—and you know how they feel about it."

Ashley's head was resting on his arm as they walked and he talked to her hair.

"I know how important it is to you that our family goes to church, and I'm happy to, but that's just not something they're interested in."

She mumbled her answer, but a deep sincerity filled her words, "Well, yeah, but it's not just that I want them to come. I love your parents and your whole family, and I don't want anything to happen to—"

Josep cut in to ease the mood, "Ahem!"

Ashley looked up at him with her puppy dog eyes. "What?"

He forced a stern look deep into her eyes. He waited a moment until she got the message.

She continued, "And you!"

Again, he cut her off, "Me, what?"

She stopped their walking and faced him properly. Their eyes locked, and the jovial smiles fell away and were replaced with a true and yearning passion. She rested a hand on his cheek and said the words the same as she had the first time, "I love you." They fell into an impassioned kiss. The world around them danced by as if it wasn't even there. Had the heartless march of time allowed, they would've stayed there forever. After what had been nearly a minute, though it had only just begun to the both of them, they reluctantly pulled away. Life demanded they return to the waking world despite how they longed to resist it. They stared at each other a few precious moments more before Josep again tried to ease them into reality with a joking, "Good."

Ashley chuckled and locked her arm under his again. They continued their walk through the parking lot. It took a few seconds for her to regain her train of thought, and she continued, "You know I love all of you so much. I just want the best for them and eventually…" Her voice trailed off as she tried to find the words. This wasn't the first time this exact conversation had taken place. Neither of them could recall the exact count. Here was where she lost the words and couldn't seem to find them.

Josep spoke for her, "I know, sweetheart. That's just how you are. You want to help save everyone, and that's great. But really, you don't have to worry about them. If it's meant to happen, they'll come around, but it's not the end of the world if they don't right away. It's not like they're opposed to any of it. They just…" Josep himself struggled to say the right words in these situations. In actuality, he wasn't concerned with it in the least. Ashley was particular about the way certain things were done. He was sensitive to that, though, and wanted to make her feel as such. He finished with what sounded best to him, "They just aren't ready yet."

It was obvious when she spoke about it that Ashley wanted to be more eloquent. To any observer, she seemed as sociable as anyone you could meet. Privately, though, she easily became frustrated with a difficulty to find the words she wanted when it came to this subject. Without another way to say it, she resorted to what she usually went to, "It's just that Jesus has influenced everything about my life, and I want to be able to share that with them. I just wish I knew some way to say that in a way they would listen to."

Josep knew her intentions were pure, but some small part of him pitied her commitment to her strict mindset. "They know, baby. They do. You do a great job of sharing your passion for God with everyone you meet. I just hate to see you stress about it so much, like you're not doing enough, or you're doing it badly. I don't know anyone else who talks about it with such an honest, open heart the way you do. They just have a different way of doing things."

He could tell from her expression that he wasn't getting anywhere. It seemed as if he never did. It wasn't a real issue to him; he knew that his parents and family were religious, and obviously, Ashley and her family were. All of them were good to go in that department. He really only felt bad for her. Countless times, and in countless ways, he'd tried to ease her mind so she wouldn't have it weighing on her, but that nagging thought in her mind apparently refused to relent. There was something in her that compelled her to keep harping on the same note over and over. She had said it a thousand times, but something about it didn't sit right with her, and so it repeated over and over.

He wanted more than anything to ease her mind. They'd vetted churches together every time they moved; they'd talked about it endlessly. It just wasn't enough that they did everything right; they had to do this one specific thing that Ashley couldn't help but come back to over and over. He couldn't figure out how to free her from that nagging tug in her heart.

She was twiddling with her fingers still as they got to the car. He walked her to the passenger door and put his hand on the handle without opening it. She stood for a moment before wondering what had stopped him. They stared into each other's eyes yet again, and the world fell away. The light swirled and danced around her. That hint of sadness in her face filled him with a swelling sense of love. He put his hands on her cheeks and slowly pulled her close until their faces were inches apart. They stood in silence, feeling each other's warmth. The warm sun rested on their skin. The gentlest breeze played with Ashley's dress. Seconds and years were as one. Josep finally broke the silence. Nothing else mattered but this, "Don't ever worry, Ashley. No matter what happens, we'll always be together. I'll never let you go. Nothing will ever keep us apart. I love you." He pulled her in before things went dark, and he awoke.

THIRTEEN

Josep was asleep. His head was spinning but slowly righted itself as his senses returned to him. It was cold. The air was dank and humid, like he was in a cave. And it was very, very dark. His body demanded rest, and he was inclined to allow it until he heard a noise nearby, and he forced himself to open his eyes. He couldn't see anything at first. His eyes slowly adjusted to the darkness until he could make out the faintest glow highlighting the edges of the rocks around him. He was in a cave, or something like it. He could just barely see, far above him, a dim pink pinhole. It was far too minor to cast any useful light down here, but the sight reminded him of where he was and where he had been.

His mind began to rush back to him now. How was he alive? Was he safe? How long had it been? Then he recalled the noise that had stirred him from his slumber. Something was moving nearby. He wasn't sure if he should get up and run or lie still and play dead. Perhaps whatever it was wouldn't notice him. His eyes strained in the dark until he saw the flicker of a brighter light bouncing off the cavern walls around the corner. This light seemed bizarre in its normalcy; a warm yellow light cascaded off the rocks and rapidly flooded the chamber.

Josep looked around quickly as the room brightened. He had been lying in the middle of the empty room, and there was nothing to hide behind. The chamber was small and had only one way in or out. The source of light was nearly upon him. He could hear slow footsteps slapping against the stone floor. He began an effort to scramble for cover, but there was none to be found. He stood to his feet and spun around but quickly conceded there was nothing he could do. Trapped in his dead end, he awaited whatever horror would appear.

The light slowly moved closer and closer until a figure turned the corner and slid into view. Whoever it was, they were small and unassuming. Josep could see the ends of stringy, gray hair peeking out from under the massive hood. A dark, turquoise cloak covered almost every inch of the stranger. A frail, gnarled hand held an oil lantern aloft. Bare feet popped in and out of view as the hooded figure stepped closer. They stopped at the entrance to Josep's tiny prison. Without a word, the two simply listened to the subtle crackling of the lamp.

Josep was nervous, but his heart rate began to slow after a minute without apparent danger. He couldn't see the stranger's face or make out any other useful details about them. The hooded figure stood unmoving, like a statue frozen in time. Josep was hesitant to make the first move, but he figured he had no real alternatives if in fact he was in danger. He thought about what he should say, but nothing seemed more helpful than "Who are you?" His voice was soft. He was fearful that he might be attacked at any moment, but his voice came out softer than he had intended. There was no sense of danger from this person. If anything, he felt like he was safer now than he had been since this whole thing started. Perhaps it was the gentle light they stood in. Unlike the terrible fires from below or the eerie pink lights that were now synonymous with danger in his mind, this glow was kind and soft. Somehow, though, at the same time, it felt cold and empty.

Moments had passed again in silence, and the stranger seemed to have no intention of answering. Perhaps they didn't understand his language. He tried to pry any kind of sound out of them to see what they could say. "Hello? Where am I? What's your name?"

Each question was met with silence. The stranger was either ignoring his questions or couldn't understand them. The quiet and the calm were at odds with the sense of urgency that was returning in Josep's heart. He was tired and had noticed a rather strong ache in his back and shoulder, but in spite of the massive fall, he was otherwise unharmed. He had given up understanding how his body worked now and was simply grateful to be alive. Ashley was still waiting, though; and if this person truly wasn't a threat, maybe they could help.

He asked another question without expecting an answer, "I'm looking for my wife, Ashley. Do you know where I can find her?"

There was another gap of stoic silence, and Josep was about to give up waiting for an answer. Suddenly, though, the figure stirred. Without saying a word, they took a step back and turned to leave the way they came. Hope began to swell in Josep yet again, but it had been dashed too many times in the past for him to trust it. He watched intently, hoping they would give some sort of clarification. Was this in answer to his question, or were they leaving for another reason? He had no idea if they even understood him.

He asked again, less for an answer and more for himself, "Do you want me to follow you? Hello?"

The figure shuffled away, dragging its feet as it went. The light had just turned the corner before Josep dared to move forward. He had no other options even if he waited to be alone, and he preferred to stay in the silent figure's lamp light rather than wander the darkness again.

Josep began down the tunnel, keeping a distance at first. The ceiling was just above his head, and the uneven floor provided poor footing. The narrow corridors wound left and right, turning back on itself and ramping up and down slopes with no sense of purpose, but there were no alternate routes along the way; a single long tunnel led from where Josep had landed to wherever it was going. As the walk dragged on, Josep dared to follow the figure a bit closer. There was no chance of losing them; they weren't so much walking as they were shambling. Josep took one step for every three the hooded figure did. As he watched the way they move and seeing the bits of them that escaped the fabric of the cloak, he knew they were very old. The wispy strands of hair that dangled this way and that seemed like a woman's to him. If it was a woman and not some creature in disguise, he would be very grateful indeed.

He dared not touch her, attempt to remove the hood, or even crouch down to look up into her face. That morbid curiosity did call to him, but he decided he'd learned his lesson and forced those urges into submission. Time passed until they'd been walking nearly half an hour. Questions came to Josep's mind. Some made sense given the circumstances, but he'd already asked those. "Who are you," "Where are we," "Where are we going," and "How can I find Ashley" to name a few.

Other thoughts came to mind that made Josep question himself again. He had realized his journey had begun to impact his thoughts some time ago, but again, it made him question why. Perhaps it was the gentle flicker of the lamp, the quiet, calm atmosphere, or simply because he missed it more now than ever before; but he began to reminisce about his life. Everything from his final years all the way back to his childhood came to mind seemingly at random. Images of memories he'd cherished his whole life rippled on the walls of the tunnel as the two strolled in silence. Memories of camping as a child, sitting by the campfire, and looking at the stars. He'd always preferred to stay indoors when he could, but every so often, nature displayed a certain majesty that no one could deny. Seldom did he think of his life before Ashley. Not because it was particularly unpleasant, but his life after he met her was a whole new world of joy.

The memories he saw now were nostalgia-fueled stories of simpler times. He could so clearly recall now the smell of smoke as he roasted marshmallows above the first fire he made with his father. His mother would sing soft, beautiful melodies as the wind blew through the trees. In a strange way, he felt the same sort of comfort now. The lamp light crackled ever so softly. He thought if only a breeze would blow by now, he might even be able to call this stroll pleasant. Without thinking, he nearly began to hum a tune himself. There was something about this that reminded him of his life in a very fond way. But that was all behind him now. This wasn't a hike through the woods with his family. His lips were cracked and constantly on the verge of bleeding. His breathing was shallow as deeper breaths burned his dusty throat. His back and shoulder were throbbing. And the damned stagnant air grated on his nerves. He'd never appreciated the wind in life the way he did in death. It was relatively cool as they traversed the tunnel, but the air was so painfully still. He'd thought to ask a number of new questions as they went, but it never seemed appropriate. Josep suspected they either couldn't speak or wouldn't, and so he didn't press any further. After another ten minutes of meandering, he heard the distant rumble of thunder echo down the tunnel; they were nearing the end.

As the exit of the tunnel approached, that faint nostalgic feeling faded away, and the world grew dimmer still. The air heated up but stopped short of the seething heat Josep expected. The smell of sulfur grew thick again. Thunder cracked far more often and far closer now than it had been. There was no dancing orange glow from below. As the opening came into view, and he could see the outside, a wave of gloom fell thick upon his spirit. Where he had been above and then below the storm clouds before, now he was in the thick of the thunderhead. There was a dim, burnt orange glow coming from somewhere he couldn't locate. He assumed it had to be the fires far below, but if that was the source, he now stood farther away from them than he ever had.

All around, red bolts arced here and there, making loud roars as they did. The searing glow spread through the clouds and illuminated the space with a bright light for only a moment at a time. The only thing ahead of him was a long, narrow bridge similar to the ones he had crossed before, only this was far more dilapidated; bits were missing here and there and had fallen off into the dark, swirling clouds below. The bridge must have led somewhere, but Josep couldn't see it from here. Dark mists hovered across the stone bridge and made it seem as if it led to nowhere at all.

Josep stood gawking until he realized the figure leading him had stopped. Together, they had walked to the edge of the cave and stood on a small ledge that sat next to the bridge. Josep waited on them to continue leading him, but the stranger made no such attempts. The two stood in silence as the lightning ominously danced about them. A bolt struck the wall of the cliff near where the two were standing, and Josep reeled back. To his surprise, the wall of the cave and the stranger hadn't flinched; it seemed both had been through this far more than once. After he'd calmed himself, Josep reluctantly accepted the task before him. The figure continued to stare unwavering out into the void. The call to move on latched on to Josep's heart, and he took a deep breath. Before he left, he took a few moments more to stand by the hooded stranger and enjoy the peace. Even among the other humans he'd met on his journey, there were no pleasant experiences. The ever-present dangers or the air of despair and torment had made every encounter a purely bitter experience. This was truly the first time since his quest began that he'd felt any real comfort.

He stood there and soaked up its last drops on the precipice of doom. Josep glanced at them again. He wished he could know who they were, but then again, it really didn't matter. He noticed then that the frail hand holding the lantern was now quivering. Pity swelled in his soul. What kind of existence was this for a person? Could someone like this, whose presence was nothing but calm and serene, truly be deserving of an eternity in this place? What had they done in life to deserve it?

Josep began to extend a hand to comfort them but stopped short. His attempts to help those he'd met had only caused more harm than good. That wasn't something he wished to repeat, especially for this wounded stranger. He pulled his hand away and turned to face the abyss in front of him. Josep took another sharp breath and pushed himself out onto the bridge.

The bridge was narrow and thin and worn. It seemed almost a mistake to call it a bridge; it was more of a sliver of stone attached to the cliff Josep was walking away from. The floor was uneven; chunks had broken off, leaving holes he had to avoid. The thing was only a few feet across. Had a strong wind come by, he could've very well fallen into the nothingness below. But of course, there was no wind to be found. The storm swirled around him like a vortex without so much as a faint gust. His real fear now was that another bolt of red light would crash against the bridge, and that would be the end.

He walked slow and half crouched to help steady himself. Josep was contemplating, crawling on all fours just to be safe, and had the bridge been only a bit more narrow, he would've done just that. After he'd made it a fair distance, he glanced behind to see his progress. He could just see the silhouette of the hooded figure, still standing where he'd left her. Their gentle, yellow light a beacon in the evil darkness. Had he not been so dead set on the prize, Josep might've gone back and resigned himself to living in the calm of that tunnel. Ashley awaited. He returned to his balance beam and slowly made his way farther out into the mist. After only a few dozen yards, he was completely lost in the clouds. The bridge disappeared into the distance behind and ahead of him. As if he was floating on nothing, lightning flashed above and below, lighting his way in the worst way possible. He had grown more accustomed to the bridge's poor footing, however, and was almost upright now. A hesitant foot stretched out before he dragged the other behind. Every few yards, he'd glance up and strain to see if the end was in sight. It only took another few minutes before he did. Josep lifted his gaze and could see a shape in the clouds. The haze slowly passed by. As it finally cleared, Josep's eyes went wide. Floating out in the clouds, attached to the stone string Josep was walking on, was a house. His house. He stared in disbelief. The pale blue paint with an off-white trim. The row of rose bushes he tried and failed to groom for years. The ornate birdhouse Ashley had built to distract from his bushes. The single missing shingle from the far-right edge of the roof. The floral drapes covered the upstairs window. The only thing missing were the wind chimes on the patio. As if it had been plucked from the rest of the world and suspended in space, it sat hovering over an empty, swirling nothing. This was it; Ashley was here.

Josep took a step forward and nearly tumbled off the ledge. His foot had fallen perfectly in a deep imprint. He steadied himself and looked at where he had tripped. There was a footprint in the stone. It was dull and smooth as if it had been slowly eroded after centuries of traffic stepping in that same place, wearing it away. He then inspected the entire bridge more closely and thought the same could be said of the whole thing, the poor footing due to countless eons of heavy usage. He didn't know what to make of it. He didn't care either.

Watching his steps more carefully, he moved as fast as he safely could toward the house. Once he had moved close enough, he called out, "Ashley!" As he did, his voice was swallowed up by a bolt of lightning. He cried out again and again. She had to be here. There were no lights on in the house, but it was theirs. They lived their lives together in this place. Emotion began to swell within him. He was so close now. Somewhere in the darkness of the house, through one of the first-floor windows, he saw motion, a shadow stirring within. "Ashley!" he cried out again.

Josep came to the end of the stone sliver and was in his yard. He began to run for the door but stopped short when it opened. A silhouette inside stood in the doorway. Josep couldn't see their face but could see it wasn't his wife. A coarse, gruff voice cried out to him, "Go away!" The voice was an old man's. To Josep's ears, the voice was familiar though his mind refused to acknowledge it. While Josep stood in silence, trying to think of the words, the man cried out again, "Leave! And don't come back!"

He had come too far. This was a trick. Some illusion. Josep stood his ground. "Is Ashley here?"

"No. Now go back!" The voice was stern but strained and worn.

Josep hesitated before he dared the question. Another red light flashed, and for a moment the man's face could be seen. Josep forced himself to ask, "Who are you?"

"N-no one. Leave, Josep," the man stuttered for only a moment as if holding something back. Josep took a step forward, and the man cried out again, louder than before, "Stop! Don't come any closer! Leave this place! And don't come back!"

It couldn't be, but he had to ask. Josep swallowed hard, "Dad?"

The two stood in silence. Lightning flashed here and there, shaking the flimsy ground they stood on. Josep was close enough to see just a bit more now. The man's haggard beard. His frame was broad, but his strength had left him. As if malnourished far longer than any human could survive, he was only a shell of the man he had been in life. Tattered cloth hung over his body. He was holding something in his hand Josep couldn't see. The man's lip trembled before he could answer, "Y-yes. It's me, son."

Josep was dumbfounded. His hands began to shake without his realizing it.

Josep's father continued, "Now leave. Please."

An avalanche of questions crowded Josep's mind. He nearly fell to his knees under the weight, but his spirit resisted. His very soul refused to accept it. This wasn't his father. It couldn't be. He knew where his father was. Strangers Josep couldn't say anything about, but he knew his father. He was a good man. A shining example. Josep didn't know about the others, but his father didn't deserve to be here. Something was wrong. Something was very wrong. It had to be a trick. Some monster in his father's form. Ashley would know. She was here. She had to be. And this thing was trying to stop him. Tears filled his eyes, but he forced himself to stand strong. "Is Ashley here?"

Josep began to step forward again, but the thing that looked like his father cried out even louder, "Stop! Josep, I'm warning you! Turn around and go back. I won't let you." He stood ready to fight and was holding a large kitchen knife out toward Josep.

It wasn't his father. It couldn't be. His father wouldn't keep them apart. Josep tested the creature, doubting every word it said, "Why? Why are you here? Why would you try to stop me? What is going on?"

The man was shaking as much as Josep now. A tear streamed down his face, but he stood firm. The burly voice escaped his with-ered body as barely more than a whisper, "I can't…I can't. Not again. Leave."

Josep took another step and was almost to the stairs that led to the patio. The beast that looked like his father summoned all its strength and let out a roar. "Stop! Leave! Now!"

It wasn't him. This wasn't his father. It wasn't. Josep walked up the stairs. The man was shaking like a leaf, unsuccessfully fighting back a river of tears that streaked down his face. Josep was less than three feet away when he couldn't hold back anymore. He shrieked like an animal and lunged forward. Josep couldn't fight his father. This couldn't be him. It wasn't. Josep jumped back and nearly fell down the stairs.

This thing that taunted him with his father's form screamed and howled. "Leave! Go!" He slashed at the air pushing Josep farther back.

He was nearly halfway down the stairs again. He couldn't go back. He was so close now. This wasn't his father. It wasn't true. Josep gripped at that thought with white knuckles. He waited for another swipe of the knife and then dove forward. The man fought like a rabid animal, without any precision but holding nothing back. Josep had never fought with his father even once. The thought made him sick to his stomach and closed his throat. He couldn't think about it. This wasn't him. He just had to get past. He shoved the man back, but he stood firm.

The man steadied himself immediately and came forward again. Josep went to grab the arm that held the knife. Even if this thing wasn't his father, something kept him from wanting to hurt it. That hesitation cost him, though. He missed the arm and the knife slashed his hand deep. Josep yelped and reeled back, clenching his hand. He managed to keep himself from tumbling down the stairs and instead slid to the side along the patio. A stream of blood poured down his arm. The image of his father gave him no time to rest. His coarse voice strained harder still, and the screams became even less human.

Over and over, he bellowed, "Get away! Go! Don't come back again!" He continued to slash wildly at the air as he ran toward Josep.

Each time, Josep backpedaled more and more. Josep was looking for something to defend himself with, but nothing useful was in sight. He turned to run around and follow the patio to the backside of the house. The man in his father's skin ran after him but was weak and slow enough to give Josep time to build some distance. Josep made it to the backdoor as the man was just turning the final corner. Josep dashed inside and closed the door behind him. He slid the deadbolt in place and wasted no time running for a weapon.

This was his and Ashley's home. The house was a small, two-story structure. The first floor was laid out like a ring with one hall dividing it down the middle, the kitchen on one side, the living room on the other. It was just as he'd left it before he died. Everything was in its place. His gun should be too. There was a pistol in the nightstand beside their bed and a shotgun in the closet by the front door.

The monster banged against the backdoor for a few seconds raging loud, "Josep! No! Stop!" It took only a few seconds for the man to scream and begin to run around the patio to the front.

Josep turned through the kitchen and to the front hall. He made it to the front door in time and slid that lock in place as well. For a moment, Josep was tempted to wait there, but the man didn't even make it to the front door to test it. From the front door, Josep could see the window in the living room sliding open and the emaciated monster frantically crawling inside. Without any time to waste, Josep continued to the closet door only a few feet away and threw it open. Inside was everything he'd left: his and Ashley's coats, her purse and scarf, their shoes lining the floor, and the butt of the shotgun resting in the corner. He pushed the coats aside and grabbed the gun. Behind it was a box of shells. He buried his hand in it and grabbed a handful.

"Josep!" the man sounded like some beast; his voice was loud and just around the corner.

Josep barely pulled himself away from the closet in time to see the man turn the corner. The beast slid across the floor on the rug by the front door, rushing like a madman. Josep ran down the hall scrambling to load the gun while he ran. He dropped a shell as he turned the corner back into the kitchen. With far more force than he needed, he snapped open the break action so he could load the gun. He was dripping in sweat now but didn't notice. His heart was pounding in his chest, and his hands were shaking so badly he could barely keep a grip on anything. He dashed around the island in the center of the kitchen to make more space. He fumbled to place the two shells he'd held onto one at a time in each barrel. As soon as he'd finished, the man turned the corner and raced toward him without a second's hesitation.

"Get out!" He shrieked as he dashed to move around the island.

Josep pulled the shotgun up as quick as he could and fired in a panic. The shot exploded off the countertop and splayed across the room. Glass shattered, and the explosion rang out just as another bolt of lightning did outside. The man had fallen on the floor behind the island and was out of Josep's sight. A tense quiet fell on the room. Thunder shook the house, and glassware tinkled throughout the kitchen as it did.

Josep stood frozen, waiting on a sound. After a few moments, he slowly tiptoed to the right to see around the island, his finger still ready to let loose another blast. His heart was filled with a tornado of emotions. This wasn't his father. It couldn't have been. But his voice and his face were just as he remembered. It couldn't be, though. His father would never try to hurt him. This…thing was something else. It had to be.

Josep slowly turned the corner, and an empty floor came into view. The man wasn't there. Josep turned left and right, scanning the room, but didn't see a thing. Somehow, he'd slipped away, and Josep had lost sight of him. Josep tensed up again, feverishly turning this way and that. He was somewhere close by, this murderous fiend. Josep turned back to look toward the front door. He thought maybe the man had slipped back into the hall and was trying to come up behind him. A second later, the man screamed right behind Josep. Before he could finish turning to face him, he felt a cold, sharp blade bury itself in his back. Josep yelled out a cry of pain. The knife was low and embedded deep in his flesh. In life, he may have fallen right there, but this strange new body was far stronger, and he managed to keep himself on his feet.

144

Josep turned toward the man and tried to aim his gun. The creature had let go of the knife and grabbed at Josep's gun. The two wrestled and pushed each other back and forth. They crashed into the walls and into the furniture. A shelf fell off the wall, and a framed picture of Josep and his father shattered on the hardwood floor. Josep stepped on a shard of glass as they fought and lost his footing as he did. He struggled to keep himself upright and smashed into the wall. The two rolled into the hallway and onto the floor. The man fought with all his feral might, but his body was far too weak to contend with Josep under normal circumstances. However, with the knife in his back, fatigue he'd endured to reach this place, and the glass cuts in his feet, Josep was nearly evenly matched with this shadow of his father. He didn't want to fight.

The two were crying and screaming like a pair of animals fighting to the death. The man was on top of Josep now, wrestling with the gun. He had returned to his grizzled plea. "Please! Josep, Leave! Not again!"

Josep didn't listen. He couldn't. This wasn't his father. Ashley was counting on him. He wouldn't leave her for anything. Josep was fighting to stay upright but was nearly on his back, and the knife was digging in, pressing against the floor. He didn't want to, but he had no choice. If he didn't fight with all he had, this animal would kill him. He couldn't fail. Josep roared with everything he had. He jerked to his side, nearly throwing the man off and giving him just enough time to deliver a strong kick to the man's gut. This broke his grip on the gun and pushed him back. With only a second to spare, Josep aimed the gun and pulled the trigger. The man flew back and landed hard on the floor down the hall.

Josep dropped the gun immediately and reached around to pull the blade out of his back. He could just barely get a good enough grip to slide it out without twisting it more. Each inch was terrible pain, but he pushed through until it finally came loose and fell to the floor. Blood pooled on the floor around him and covered his hands. He grunted against the pain. His body wanted to give out, but somehow, he gathered the strength to stand again. He was hesitant until he saw his father's form. The man was lying flat on his back, a massive hole in his abdomen. His eyes were fixed on the ceiling above him. Tears flowed down his cheeks. Blood filled the hallway.

Josep couldn't stand upright and was leaning against the wall. He was breathing heavily. His mind was a blur. The sight of his father in such a state nearly made him vomit. He continued to repeat in his mind over and over that it wasn't him. His father was nothing like this. Nothing in life had ever pushed them to something like this. Josep loved his father, and his father loved him. Both his parents and he were very close until the day they died. Neither of them could end up in a place like this. Josep knew where they were, and it wasn't here. They never deserved this. They were saints. Good people. This wasn't him, dying on the floor.

Josep looked at the stairs on the other side of the man. Josep tried to cry out, but it was only a murmur, "Ashley." He began to stumble down the hall. He stepped through the puddle of blood that surrounded the man. Josep tried not to look at him and stepped over his arm. He couldn't help but hear the man mumbling with his last breaths, though. Over and over, the man repeated the same thing, "Not again…not again."

Josep refused to think about it. He had to ignore the questions and emotions assaulting his mind. If he gave them an inch, they would stop him dead in his tracks. It didn't matter anyway. What mattered was Ashley. She was here. It was time to save her. He pulled himself away, his heart like a brick in his chest. Slowly, he slid himself to the stairs. With all his weight against the railing, he pulled himself, hand over hand up each step, leaving bloody handprints as he went. This wouldn't kill him. Somehow, he could tell. He needed rest and to stop the bleeding, but first, he had to find Ashley. The sight of her would heal any wound at this point. His mind would be at ease. Finally, it would all make sense, and he could let go. He was nearly at the top when he cried out again, using all his energy to force out her name, "Ashley!" After what felt like an eternity, he made it to the landing. To his right was their bedroom, and he moved there instinctively.

The door was closed. He put his hand on the knob and fell into it with all his weight. The door flew open and slammed against the wall.

"Ashle—" His cry was cut short at what he saw inside. The room was just as he remembered. Everything where he'd left it. Two shapes were laying in the bed under the sheets. He couldn't see the faces but he knew who it was. There was a chair across the room from the bed by the window. The curtains were drawn, and the room was dark. A shadowy figure sat in the chair with their legs crossed. The room was dead silent as if the storm outside was a very distant thing. The shadows seemed to come alive in some unexplainable way. There was a pressure in the air. Something heavy and thick weighing on him. Josep stood in silence, leaning against the open door. He looked at the figures under the sheets and back at the shrouded figure in the chair. The figure waited, letting the tension build. Then, just before Josep could say a word, a silvery voice broke the silence. It was sweet and lustrous, strong and regal, yet cold and empty. The words slithered from the shadow and into Josep's mind, "Welcome back, Josep."

A pang of recollection hit Josep like another knife, a sense of déjà vu so powerful it was almost violent. A splinter dug into his mind and nearly knocked him off his feet. Suddenly, the vortex of emotions he had been suppressing went quiet. The questions came one at a time, orderly and neat. Josep's face was pale as he spoke, "Who are you?"

The figure rose to their feet. The shadow stood a head taller than Josep, their head nearly reaching the ceiling. They walked to the curtains with the grace of royalty. With both hands, they threw the curtains aside, letting the dim, nightmarish light flood the room. A bolt of lightning flashed by the window, but the sound seemed to be a million miles away. The room was still, like a graveyard. The light from outside outlined the man's bare body. His shoulders were broad and powerful. He stood like a giant. Long, flowing blond hair hung halfway down his back and draped over his shoulders. It seemed to somehow sparkle even in the gloomy light. His pale skin seemed almost pearlescent. He stood with his back to Josep for a few moments, letting the silence sink in before choosing to answer. His voice was almost musical, a somber and ominous tune, "You still don't remember?"

He was real. He wasn't a concept or a metaphor or some exaggerated thing. He was physical and imposing and standing in the room. The air had been stagnant since Josep had entered hell. That fact had weighed on his mind and spirit and body for a very long time now. In this room, it was all the more so; somehow, it felt like the air itself had frozen in a fearful reverence if there was any air at all. The pain in Josep's back was burning. He could feel a warm wetness running down from the wound to his leg. He heaved with each breath but couldn't seem to get any air in his lungs. He felt like he was suffocating, but he continued to speak, "Why are you here?"

The man turned to face Josep. His eyes seemed to glow with a pale, golden light, like a wild cat in the night. Their eyes locked, and an otherworldly sense of dread began to bubble up inside Josep, sitting heavy in his stomach and rising to his chest.

The man spoke, and his silky voice danced around the room before settling in Josep's ear, "The question is, why are you here? Isn't that far more important?"

Josep knew why he was here and didn't hesitate to answer, "Ashley. Where is she?"

"I already told you, Josep."

The man's mouth closed, and another voice came from behind. Another voice that rang a loud bell in Josep's mind. A whisper, right in his ear, "She is not here."

Josep turned his head toward the voice, back toward the hall. There was no one there. It was just the two of them. The voice spoke again in his other ear, always from behind, "She's not here, Josep. She never will be."

Josep looked around frantically. The voice wasn't in the room. It echoed in his mind, taunting him, whispering lies and truths that he couldn't distinguish. The conversation from so long ago repeated in his head over and over. "She isn't here... You know why... She never will be... What did you do?"

The splinter in Josep's mind dug in deeper, cracking his fragile spirit. His breathing quickened, and his eyes felt moist. It didn't matter. Only one thing did. Josep asked again, "Where is she?"

The man took a few steps toward the bed, almost as if he was floating across the room. His body was perfect. The light wrapping around his muscular form. A hazy, golden trail flowed from his eyes. He spoke like a man trying to hide his delight, "Oh, don't try to rush it so fast, Josep. This is my favorite part. This is what I look forward to every time. And you certainly took your sweet time this go around, as well. You had to start again quite a few times. I do hope you aren't losing the fire that made me so interested in you, to begin with."

A white noise began to fill Josep's mind. He struggled to formulate thoughts. His mind felt stretched and thin. He asked, "What is this?"

"You know the answer to that one, Josep. This is the end. And the beginning. This is when you start another lap. Or did you want me to explain it to you?" The man was refined and composed, but his voice betrayed a subtle child-like giddiness. He continued, "You died a long time ago, Josep. You and Ashley both have been dead for far longer than your feeble mind can comprehend. Though it seems now like the blink of an eye. You've seen every possible path from your start to this finish line so many times. You're a celebrity. People see you walking down the road, and a viral cloud of despair comes with you. You're a symbol of the perfect failure. You had everything right at your fingertips, and you fumbled. You missed the goal, and you landed right in my lap. For that, I am truly grateful." He took a royal bow; the sarcasm was enough to choke on. The man took another step and reached the edge of the bed. He rested a hand on the sheets and then looked down at the shapes in the bed. "I've said it before, Josep, but I mean it more every time I say it." He took a few moments to observe the still forms before turning back to Josep. "You are so very fun to watch."

Josep didn't have any thoughts. His mind was a blank. The white noise was so loud now it filled his head and blocked out any thoughts of his own that might come about. As if he was being fed which questions to ask, the next left his mouth, "Why?"

A beautiful and sickening grin appeared on the man's face. "You're special, Josep. Most humans don't know what it means to care for anything at all. They think they do, but they couldn't comprehend just how little they do. Very few humans truly care about anything. Usually a meaningless thing. Useless vapors. But it's that caring that's special. Even fewer still care about something so much they would give their lives for it. They cling to their lives with all their pathetic might, and yet they would give it up for something even less meaningful than them. But you're even rarer still. You care beyond your life. You've given your life, over and over and over, and you still care. You care just as much as the day you started caring. You bare your soul and offer it a living sacrifice to your own personal goddess. A dull, broken idol who ended up in the same place as you. Now, I think that caring matters, Josep." The shimmering man stepped around the bed and toward Josep. Each step Josep felt smaller and smaller. His tone slowly swelled revealing a passion more titanic than anything Josep's mind could comprehend. "I value that caring. No matter how many times I test you, you keep getting up and doing the same thing with the same fighting spirit as before. You don't give up. You don't stop. Even though you should have so very long ago. You want it so badly you would sell your soul to whoever asked if it meant having your goddess back. I've seen you tear your own beating heart out of your chest because you thought it meant saving her. You are possessed by your zealous worship, and I bathe in that glorious display every time, Josep! If you weren't such a pathetic waste of dust, I might even be impressed." The man stood a foot away now, towering over Josep.

Somehow Josep wasn't standing by the door anymore. The room was much larger than it had been. The only thing around Josep was the bed, the window, the chair, and the man. Everything else was black and cold and empty.

"And what did you get for all your devotion? What reward did your ceaseless prayer earn you?" The man leaned down, and his presence pushed Josep into the floor.

Josep fell to his knees. His spirit dried up. Tears rolled down his cheeks as familiar despair consumed him.

"You get to bask in my presence. You crawl on your hands and knees and worship your goddess, and I take it as a song to my glory. For all eternity, you will continue to chase your hollow prize, and your boundless suffering will bring me endless delight." The man stood and spread his arms wide, soaking in Josep's torment. "I find your offering most satisfying, my humble acolyte!"

Suddenly the man was holding Josep's throat and holding him aloft. He moved faster than light itself, and it was over before Josep realized it had begun. "Now do it again. I want more."

The room jerked and twisted. A red flash of lightning exploded outside and inside and everywhere else. The thunder boomed and shrieked and crackled, and Josep thought he had died again. Maybe he had. What did it matter now? Suddenly, the world was back, and Josep was kneeling in the foyer of the prison. The shining pale man standing like a titan among insects in front of him. His eyes were flaming now. A roaring, monstrous golden flame that made his body shine even darker. Josep could hear the jailers approaching. They were cackling and howling and jeering. The bloody red brute was leading the river and rushing to be the first. They would be on him soon.

The splinter in Josep's mind had shattered everything. It was over. And it never would be. Here he would remain as he always had. Memories of the torture flashed in the white noise of his mind. He had endured so much and failed to endure far more. He'd died over and over. Each time awakening anew to start it all over. Each time with the sole purpose of finding his love. To find Ashley. It didn't matter now. But it was the only thing that could. He was emptied and hollow. He couldn't bring himself to scream or cry. It had been too many eons. For a few more hours, he would remember everything. And then he would remember nothing. Doomed to forget, only so he could come to the realization as fresh as when he'd first begun. It didn't matter, but he had to ask. With the end of his strength, he asked one last time, "Where is she?"

The silvery, dark prince looked down with a smile so satisfied and prideful. The look told a wicked tale that promised suffering and torment beyond human comprehension. It was worse than what Josep could've ever dared to imagine. She was gone forever. He would never see her again. And he would never stop trying.

TWO

Ashley was awake. More awake than she'd ever been. She was finally alive. The air was searing with a glorious and beautiful heat. Her skin tingled at its touch. The sound of majestic wind chimes danced on the wild and wondrous breeze. When she'd first opened her eyes, the pain was unbearable, and yet it was over in a flash. Heavy scales fell to the ground, and for the first time in her life, she could truly see. Colors she'd never imagined made up only the tiniest details, and the rest was beyond words. It was bright. Bright and golden and blinding. Here, there could be no shadows. There was no room anymore. The Light was everywhere. Whereas in life she had sat near lights, now she rested in the only real light. The sky stretched to infinity, and still, it wasn't nearly enough to contain the whole. The purple and blue and pink and ultraviolet clouds swirled everywhere, too overjoyed to stand still for even a moment.

When she awoke, there were questions. So many questions. And yet, so few that mattered. Suddenly, things were clear. Everything made sense in a way that it never had before. Now she stood before a figure of dazzling, heated bronze that took her breath away. She fell to her knees in awe and wonder as more realizations washed over her. Something else that became clear was that Josep had not come with her. She cried her tears. Many tears. But she stood in the presence of Peace. And at the end of her crying, His glowing hand, with heat like the sun, wiped the tears from her cheeks. They fell to the golden ground and were no more. The Man stood beside her as she entered the gates. Her case was pleaded for her, and despite her crimson robe, she appeared as snow. It was the end. And the beginning. Now her real life had begun. And it would never end.

She had lived there for more time than time itself. The experiences of a thousand lifetimes passed in the blink of an eye. And now, she was here. She sat at a table and had just finished her story.

"And then I woke up."

The woman across from her spoke first, "What a beautiful story, Ashley. It sounds so strange to be in a place where His presence isn't physical."

Ashley responded, "Well, in a way it was. I see that now. But during my time, it did seem as if He was distant at times. Even though He was there all along, it was something I had to remind myself was true. Not like how you and Dagar saw Him. That still gives me chills to think about."

The man next to the woman answered as Ashley took a drink, "It was strange to appreciate it as little as we did. In some ways, I wish I had the chance to experience Him the way you did. The idea of His spirit actually dwelling inside you during your time is extraordinary to try to imagine."

Another man at the other end of the table spoke up, "I wonder how it would compare to the way we felt Him. To us, He wasn't physical either, not until near the end." He gestured to the two men who looked just like him that sat on either side. "But like you described, Ashley, we could always feel Him if we tried. He made Himself known to us if we would just humble ourselves and remember to seek Him."

Ashley finished her drink. "Yes, I was wondering if you three wouldn't tell your story next. You mentioned it briefly before Dagar and Eliz's, and I've been so very curious to hear it."

The man responded, "Oh. Are you sure? Personally, I still find Aadi's the most peculiar of us all."

The group looked to a much younger boy sitting to Ashley's left. He shied away at the attention but answered politely, "Well, I don't know about that."

The gathering chuckled at his reaction. The man sitting with the two like him continued, "But if you want, Ashley, we don't mind sharing next."

Before he could continue, though, another man who'd been quiet up until now rose to his feet. He spoke with a smooth voice, "I'm sorry everyone, but I'm going to have to catch up on Roy's story later. I have to get back to mine for one last time before I'm finished."

The woman across from Ashley answered first, "Oh, and Ryz's is fantastic too! And so unique."

Ashley was confused, "What do you mean go back? You mean you aren't done yet?"

The man standing answered her question, "Well, yes. To me, it seems so strange that all of you only had one time. I've been told this will be my last, but I've had many, many times before."

Ashley wanted very much to hear more, but it was obvious he had to leave, and so she didn't hold him. "Well, I'll be looking forward to hearing all about it when you get back."

The man smiled and gave a short bow. "I'll make sure to take notes so I don't miss any details." He turned to leave, and the group bid him farewell until they saw him again.

When they had finished their goodbyes, they collectively refilled their drinks, and a few grabbed some dessert before they returned to the table. Ashley anxiously sat down and asked before she had settled, "So, Roy, do tell!"

The three men who looked alike shared a laugh together at her enthusiasm before beginning to tell their story.

About the Author

Joey Zigan was born into a military family, moving over twenty times during his childhood. This living situation provided a unique perspective on life. After graduating with a degree in graphic design, he worked as an artist for Walt Disney World and Universal Studios theme parks before being called into the realm of education. However, throughout all his adventures, two things have remained constant: his Christian faith and his passion for storytelling. After writing privately for years, a friend recommended he submit his work to the Florida Christian Writer's Conference where the book you're holding won first place in the fiction category.